Before *the* Throne

Before *the* Throne

DIALOGS WITH EGYPT'S GREAT
FROM MENES TO ANWAR SADAT

Naguib Mahfouz

Translated by
Raymond Stock

The American University in Cairo Press
Cairo   New York

First published in 2009 by
The American University in Cairo Press
113 Sharia Kasr el Aini, Cairo, Egypt
420 Fifth Avenue, New York, NY 10018
www.aucpress.com

Dar el Kutub No. 4096/09
ISBN 978 977 416 291 6

Dar el Kutub Cataloging-in-Publication Data

Mahfouz, Naguib, 1911–2006
        Before the Throne / Naguib Mahfouz; translated by Raymond
    Stock.—Cairo: The American University in Cairo Press, 2009
            p.   cm.
        ISBN 978 977 416 291 6
        1. Arabic fiction   I. Stock, Raymond (trans.)   II. Title
        813

1 2 3 4 5 6 7 8   14 13 12 11 10 09

Printed in Egypt

1

THE COURT GATHERED in its divine entirety within the Hall of Justice, whose high walls were adorned with writing in the sacred hieroglyphic script, under a gilded ceiling in whose heavens gleamed the dreams of all humankind. In the center of the hall Osiris reposed on his golden throne; to his right was Isis, and to his left Horus, each seated on their own thrones. Not far from Osiris's feet squatted Thoth, Scribe of the Gods, the Book of All laid open across his thighs. Meanwhile, chairs plated with pure gold were arrayed on both sides of the hall, ready to receive those whose ultimate fates now would be written.

To commence the proceedings, Osiris declaimed, "From the remotest past, it has been decreed that humans shall spend their lives on earth. All the while, there would go with them, even over the threshold of death—like a shadow that clings to them—a record of all their acts and desires, embodied on their naked forms. Finally, there would be held a detailed dialog that would end with a decisive word. This, then, is that trial, convened after the passage of the allotted span of time."

Osiris then signaled to Horus, and the youth called out with a booming voice, "King Menes!"

From the door at the farthest end of the hall, a man entered, attired in his burial shroud, though his head and feet were bare. With clear features and a powerful form, he drew closer and closer to Osiris's throne, until he stood three arms' lengths from it, in a stance of stark humility.

1

At this, Osiris beckoned to the divine scribe Thoth, who began to read from the book before him, "The mightiest monarch of the First Dynasty, he warred on the Libyans until he subdued them. He attacked Lower Egypt, joining it to southern Egypt, declaring himself king of all Egypt together, crowning himself with the Double Crown. He altered the course of the Nile, establishing the city of Memphis on the new land this formed."

Addressing Menes, Osiris demanded, "Tell us what you have to say."

"Thoth, your sacred scribbler, has condensed my life in words," Menes replied. "How easy is the telling, and how hard was the doing!"

"We have our own view of how to appraise rulers and their deeds," Osiris warned him. "Do not waste time by praising yourself."

"I inherited rule of the southern kingdom from my family," Menes said. "With it I inherited a mighty dream—which all of our early men and women shared—to cleanse the country of foreign intruders, and establish an eternal unity whose two wings would be the lands of southern and northern Egypt.

"The voice of my paternal aunt, Awuz, was the prime moving force that ignited this awesome dream. She would gaze at me with concern and say, 'Will you spend your whole life eating, drinking, and hunting?' Or she would goad me by adding, 'Osiris did not teach us farming merely to give us a chance to fight among ourselves over the water needed to irrigate a feddan.'

"Once I said to my beloved spouse that I could feel a firebrand in my breast that would not cool until I had realized this dream. She was a splendid royal wife when she answered me with passion, 'Don't let the Libyans threaten your capital—and don't allow the people to divide up the land that the Nile has made one.'

"So I threw myself with vigor into training our strong men for battle, praying to the gods to endow me with the satisfaction of victory, until at my hand the vision of which my pioneering parents and grandparents had dreamed was fulfilled."

"You reaped one hundred thousand of the Libyans' lives," Osiris reproached him.

"They were the aggressors, My Lord," said Menes in his own defense.

"And of the Egyptians, northerners and southerners combined, two hundred thousand fell as well," Osiris reminded him.

"They sacrificed themselves for the sake of our nation's unity," said Menes. "Then security and peace reigned over all, while the blood that had regularly been shed in periodic fighting ceased to flow into the waters of the Nile."

"Could you not win the people over with words before resorting to the sword?" asked Osiris.

"I tried that with my neighbors, and brought some of them to us without going to war," Menes answered. "But afterward, the sword achieved in a few years what words had failed to do in generations."

"Many say such things merely to conceal their belief in force," said Osiris.

"The glory and security of Egypt took possession of my emotions," objected Menes.

"Your personal glory too," the presiding divinity rejoined.

"I do not deny that," Menes conceded, "but well-being was general throughout the country."

"Wherein your own dynasty and supporters benefited the most—and the peasants the least," continued Osiris.

"I spent most of my reign in combat and construction," Menes replied. "I never luxuriated in the life of the palace, nor savored the taste of fine food or drink, nor cavorted with women other than my own wife—while I was obliged to reward my helpers as befitted their labors."

Isis asked leave to speak.

3

"My Lord," she said, "you are judging a human, not a god. According to this man, he forsook ease and indolence to purge the land of invaders. He unified Egypt, freed her hidden powers, and uncovered her buried blessings. At the same time, he provided the peasants with peace and security. He is a son of which to be proud."

Osiris was silent briefly, then called out, "O King, take the first seat at the right side of the throne as your own."

Menes proceeded to his chair, knowing he was one of the privileged few who may dwell in the Other World.

2

HORUS HAILED THE COURT, "King Djoser and his vizier, Imhotep!"

From the most distant door to the hall two men, both wrapped in their winding sheets, heads and feet bare, strode briskly forward, one behind the other. The one in the lead was of medium height and solidly built. The one following was shorter and very thin. They walked until they both stood before Osiris, who spoke first to Imhotep.

"Step forward, next to the king," he said. "In this court, there is no difference between a monarch and his flock."

Imhotep carried out this command, and Thoth read out, "King Djoser, founder of the Third Dynasty. He invaded Nubia, discovered the copper mines in the Eastern Desert, and built the Step Pyramid.

"And Vizier Imhotep. A sage whose wisdom was passed on for generations. He mastered medicine, astronomy, magic, and architecture: people revered his memory for centuries after his death."

Osiris called on Djoser to speak.

"A unified kingdom—vast of expanse, plentiful in resources, and dwelling in peace—was given to me at birth. Yet those surrounding it had ambitions toward it. So I initiated a policy— followed by those who came after me—that the defense of Egypt rests on smiting those who strike her from beyond her borders. The country from which most of this infiltration into my country occurred was Nubia. As a result, I decided to expand our southern borders by invading Nubia's north, where I established a temple to the God. By virtue of his science and sorcery,

Imhotep was aware of the hidden riches in the Eastern Desert. I dispatched expeditions to explore the belly of the earth, where we were rewarded by the discovery of immense veins of copper, a material greatly useful in both war and peace. As the nation's welfare rose, I erected the Step Pyramid. At the same time, I encouraged the sciences by awarding gifts to those who excelled in them. The days of my reign brought to Egypt both strength and progress."

Osiris then summoned Imhotep to speak.

"I grew up loving science and knowledge," Imhotep began. "I studied under the august priests of Memphis, learning all that was known about medicine, engineering, astronomy, magic, and wisdom. When the king heard of my unusual erudition, he brought me to work in his royal entourage, though I was of humble origins. And I proved my worthiness in everything he charged me to do: I successfully cured the king of the illnesses that come with the desert storms of spring. Through sorcery, I saved one of the princesses from a malicious spirit and the evil eye. In reward, Pharaoh made me his minister, and commissioned me to build his pyramid. This was the construction miracle of its age, yet I would not have achieved what I did—in knowledge, expertise, or labor—if not for the divine sanction and inspiration of Ra."

"But you invaded Nubia," Osiris drilled Djoser, "without an attack being launched against you from within the borders of her kingdom."

"I have stated, My Lord," Djoser replied, "that the defense of our own borders was guided by the idea of assaulting those who came against us from outside them."

"A theory only espoused by the powerful harboring aggression," opined Osiris.

"My first duty was to prevent any probable harm to my country."

"You built a temple to the God, endowing it with lands used by those who had nothing," Osiris accused him.

"But temples have rights above all others," answered Djoser.

"That explanation does not hold without the proper consideration of the prevailing conditions."

The king lapsed into silence, as Osiris resumed his prosecution.

"You did not provide the miners with enough care and sustenance," he berated him. "Many of them perished."

"Great works are not made without victims and sacrifice," Djoser shot back.

Osiris then turned to Vizier Imhotep. "What was your opinion of the king's policies?"

"In my view," said Imhotep, "trade relations would do more than invasions to protect our borders. I thought as well that the temple's expenses should have been drawn from Egypt, and should benefit the unfortunate people of Nubia. Moreover, I did not want to send missions to the Eastern Desert until we had given them adequate provisions and medical attention. Yet my lord was eager to bolster the security and prosperity of Egypt and her people."

"Happy is he can who defend himself truthfully without shirking the defense of another," Osiris declared. "The gods did not fall short in your education—for they taught you not only the principles of farming and fighting, but of proper conduct, as well."

Isis asked to say a word.

"Djoser is a great king," she insisted, "despite his faults, and Imhotep is a beloved son who has ennobled his nation."

Osiris addressed them, "O King, I will be satisfied that I have rebuked you. Take your seats—you and your vizier—among the Immortals."

Djoser sat down on the right hand of Menes, and Imhotep to the right of Djoser.

3

"KING KHUFU!" Horus exclaimed.

The king came in, powerfully built and rather tall, bareheaded and barefoot though wound in his shroud, until he stood obediently before the throne.

Then Thoth began to read aloud, "King Khufu: chief monarch of the Fourth Dynasty; he of the Great Pyramid. He organized the state's administration with a rigor not seen either before or since. In his time, the land was abundant with goods and the markets were full, while agriculture, industry, and the arts reached their highest degree of refinement. Meanwhile, the pious awe of Pharaoh burst outward on the horizons like the sun, cowing the troublesome desert tribes, so that peace prevailed in every district and in every soul."

Asked to speak by Osiris, Khufu recounted, "From infancy I was enchanted by order and precision. All activities must have their rules and time-honored methods. In this, there is no difference between police work and sculpture, or architecture and marital relations. My personality reached into each village as an example to civil servants, the guardians of public order, and to those in the temples. Egypt became an assembly of heavenly traditions and precise administrative systems. This is what aided me in erecting the most monumental building known to man. Many thousands harmoniously took part in building it for over twenty years, a period unmarred by neglect and unrest. Not one of the laborers went without due care or protection, nor was there ever wanting a watchful, wakeful eye. And so my people boldly embarked upon a unique experiment with exemplary success, demonstrating beyond doubt their transcendent ability in the service of the God, and in gaining His satisfaction and His blessings."

"Did you exploit your nation in building your tomb?" Osiris questioned him caustically.

"If I had merely wanted a tomb for myself, then I would have had it dug out in the mountains, far beyond the sight of any covetous eye," said Khufu. "Instead, I built a symbol of divine immortality caching within it all the secrets hidden from the mind of man. The people were so keen to build it that they created a complete city—happy and holy in itself—where they labored to the utmost for the sake of the God alone. This was the work of free men—not of slaves!"

Osiris turned to his right toward that happy few who had attained eternal life in the Other World. "Let whoever wishes, speak!"

"A majestic accomplishment," lauded Menes, "that reminds me of the building of mighty Memphis, which age did not permit me to finish."

"It would have been more propitious," Djoser chided, "to direct the power at your disposal toward raids to secure the nation's borders."

"The goods of neighboring countries came to me without combat," objected Khufu. "My concern for the lives of my subjects was no less than my zeal for glory and immortality."

"Yet you took an innocent life when a man prophesied to you that a child other than your own would inherit your throne," Osiris reminded him.

"The king is obliged to protect his throne in order to defend the unity of his country," said Khufu. "And in doing so, he is bound to be right sometimes—and wrong at others."

"Were you not, in this case, defying the will of the God?"

"We do what we think duty demands, and the God does what He wills."

"Word spread that your eldest daughter fell into debauchery," Osiris told Khufu.

In a wounded tone, Khufu replied, "Sometimes the honor of even the noblest is injured without their knowledge."

"But it was said that you blessed her lewdness in order to wrench yourself from a painful predicament."

"That is pure calumny!" Khufu fumed. "Deceit has no place in this hallowed hall!"

Granted permission to speak, Isis said, "This enlightened king is like a sun in the sky of sovereign thrones. And how many vanished empires have left behind them such a towering pyramid as his? All the while, his greatness is a source of envy for the weak and incapable, both abroad, and among his own people."

At this, Osiris commanded Khufu, "Take your seat, O King, among the Immortals."

4

HORUS PROCLAIMED, "The Sage Ptahhotep!"

A short, reed-thin man entered, whose bare head and feet detracted not at all from his subtle dignity. He tread cautiously forward until he stood politely before the court.

Thoth, Recorder for the Gods, began to recite, "The Sage Ptahhotep. He lived one hundred and ten years, and served as vizier to King Izezi, one of the rulers of the Fifth Dynasty. He is the author of highly valued admonitions that achieved great acclaim."

When Osiris called upon him to speak, the wise man said, "I studied science in the temple of Ptah. My erudition was obvious, even as a child. After a long period in the priesthood, the king chose me as his minister. The days of greatness and glory had gone, as though they had never been. Those who sat on the throne were kings without power, and without wisdom as well. While they busied themselves with planning, building, and seeking to achieve their whimsical goals, the influence of the priests and the ambitions of the provincial governors for authority and to attain their own ends grew ever stronger. Corruption spread among those who held office, as the peasants were burdened with oppression and degradation. Meanwhile, the groans of complaint arose until they clogged the heavens like a fog. Over and over again, I contemplated the prevailing conditions, unable to accept them, dismayed by the darkened relations between humanity and the gods. Yet I did not stint in offering advice—which was lost in the folds of laziness and selfishness. And when

I reached my one-hundred-and-tenth year, the king summoned me and ordered me to compose a book of my choicest words of wisdom—and this I did."

"Let us hear one of your sayings," Osiris commanded.

"'If an important man invites you to supper, accept only what is offered to you, and do not speak unless you are asked to,'" said Ptahhotep.

"What provoked your interest in manners at table?"

"While apparently focusing on etiquette at meals, I was really critiquing the covetousness of the priests, who were demanding larger and larger endowments while gorging themselves on food and drink!"

"Tell us another," said Osiris.

"'Do not betray one who trusts you to bolster your glory, or to build your house,'" said Ptahhotep. "Here I was speaking of the provincial governors, who were constantly expanding their own influence—thus threatening the nation's unity."

"Had they forgotten," King Menes asked, "the blood that was shed for the sake of unifying the country?"

"And how could they spurn the traditions and the morals that were held sacred in my era?" seconded Khufu.

Osiris motioned to Ptahhotep to resume his recitation. "And you also said," he reminded the sage, "'When you enter another's house, be careful not to approach the women, for how many have met their doom that way!' Did you base that on what was said had happened in Khufu's harem?"

"To similar purpose," replied Ptahhotep, "I also said, 'If you are wise, you will put your house in order and love your wife, who is your partner in life. Feed her and clothe her; give her fragrances and bestow pleasure upon her. Do not be harsh with her, for by tenderness you will possess her heart. If her requests are granted, she will be your happiness and well-being.'"

"Give us a proverb addressed to all," commanded Osiris.

"Fail not to adorn yourself with the ornament of learning and the finery of fair behavior."

"There were no sages in my time," said King Menes. "But men freed their land from the invaders and unified their kingdom. And yet, here was an age of dissolution and corruption that produced nothing of value but some pretty words. Of what use, then, is wisdom?"

"Wisdom will endure like a pyramid—or even longer," Khufu declared.

Isis pleaded, "Do not belittle my insightful son. We are in need of the wise man in times of decline, just as we need a doctor during a plague. The sweet scent of the sound word shall linger forever."

Finally, Osiris told him, "Proceed, O Sage, to your place among the Immortals."

5

HORUS DECLAIMED with his reverberating voice, "The rebels of the Age of Darkness that fell between the collapse of the Old Kingdom and the creation of the Middle Kingdom!"

In came a group of people of varying shapes and sizes. They approached, wrapped in their shrouds but with bare heads and feet, until they lined up in single file before the throne.

Thoth, Scribe of the Gods, read a new page aloud. "These are the leaders of the revolution: they directed the angry people in a bloody, destructive revolt. They then ruled the country for the long period that lasted from the fall of the Old Kingdom to the start of the Middle Kingdom. Afterward, they left behind them nothing to mark their former presence but ruined temples, plundered tombs, and monstrous memories."

"Nominate someone to speak for you," Osiris ordered them.

They all pointed to a tall, gaunt man with a stony face.

"Abnum," they said, "for he was the first to call for disobedience and fighting!"

Osiris then called upon him to speak.

"History has neglected our names and deeds," intoned Abnum. "History remembers the elite, and we were from the poor—the peasants, the artisans, and the fishermen. Part of the justice of this sacred hall is that it neglects no one. We have endured agonies beyond what any human can bear. When our ferocious anger was raised against the rottenness of oppression and darkness, our revolt was called chaos, and we were called mere thieves. Yet it was nothing but a revolution against despotism, blessed by the gods."

"How could the gods bless aggression against sacrosanct things?" erupted Khufu.

"The tragedy began with the weakening of King Pepi II through the ravages of age," replied Abnum. "He became confused, and no longer knew what was happening around him. The governors of the provinces became independent in their nomes, and ruled autocratically over their inhabitants, imposing tyrannical taxes upon them. The priests made common cause with the governors, eager to preserve their temple estates, and so permitted them every form of evil through their fraudulent religious edicts. They paid no mind to the laments of the deprived, and their sufferings from sorrow, humiliation, and starvation. Whenever an oppressed person approached them, they demanded subservience and patience, and promised that their lot would be better in the world to come. Our despair became extreme—for no governor was just, no law was sovereign, and no justice came down to us. So I went out among my people and urged them to disobey and to fight oppression with force— and quickly they answered the call. They smashed the barrier of fear and of obsolete traditions, and dealt lethal blows to the tyrants and oppressors. The holy fire spread everywhere in the country, the missiles of burning rage raining down upon the governors, the bureaucrats, the officials of the temples and cemeteries, until we occupied the key positions of power."

"Have you not read the verses of the wise Ipuwer, which lament the loss of the sanctities, what befell the elite, and the destruction of values?" Osiris asked.

"Ipuwer was a great poet," answered Abnum. "But he was loyal to the oppressors. His tears of sadness were shed for the sons and daughters of tyrants—and he was shocked that their places were taken by the common people's children."

"You speak, Abnum," adjudged Ptahhotep, "from a standpoint of envious hatred: that is a horrendous sin."

15

"That hatred was sown in our hearts by the oppressors themselves."

"By the gods, what I'm hearing is amazing," interjected Djoser. "What was Egypt but a boat filled with sacred traditions, which capsized as a building does when a key brick loosens? Pharaoh is the divinity made flesh. The nobility are his deputies who reflect his light. The civil functionaries serve him and his subjects are the bearers of his message. How could their places be filled by a bunch of peasants, artisans, and fishermen?"

"Yet they did indeed take their positions," Abnum answered, "proving that they were better than those whom they replaced, and that the gods embody themselves in whoever raises the standard of justices and mercy, regardless of their identity."

"What impudence!" shouted Djoser.

Osiris swiveled toward him. "I will not suffer any speech that violates courtesy. Apologize."

"I offer you my apology: I am sorry," said Djoser.

"The traditions of this court permit you to take part in discussions," Osiris said to those seated in the gallery of Immortals, "but within the limits of politeness. Remember well that you might in future be addressing persons who belong to other faiths, founded after your own."

Then, turning toward Abnum, he said, "Your era was one of darkness, yet did you not leave even one monument, nor a single document, behind you?"

"That is the work of historians," pleaded Abnum. "The peasants set up a government drawn from their own sons. As they ruled the country, security was established while justice spread its reach, along with the shade of compassion. The poor were satisfied; they gained science and knowledge, filling the highest positions. The nation ascended, with no less greatness than the state of King Khufu, yet without wasting money on building pyramids or waging wars. This renaissance was financed through agriculture, industry, and the arts, plus the revival of the villages and towns. And when—after we had gone—Egypt of the pharaohs returned, they burned the papyri that recorded our deeds."

"The wisdom to build pyramids was lacking among you," rebuked Khufu.

"Nor did you have the sagacity to declare war in order to raid the lands on your borders," echoed Djoser.

"We felt it was better to educate a peasant than to throw up a temple," Abnum rebutted.

"You have spoken blasphemy," said Ptahhotep.

"The gods do not need places of worship, but the peasants need learning. That is why the gods blessed our rule for a hundred years with peace and prosperity."

"Then why did your kingdom come to an end?" asked Khufu.

"When our rulers forgot the root that had nurtured them," explained Abnum. "They dreamed, like those before them, that they were descended from the offspring of Ra. They were afflicted by pride, and darkness crept into them, until they were apprehended by that which overtakes all oppressors."

"Your wealth dissipated and crimes were committed that know no sanction by any religion, morality, or law," lamented Osiris.

"I bear witness before your justice that I personally gave no orders for any of that, nor was I ever informed of it," the leading rebel remonstrated.

"I concede that this is one of the wisest and noblest of my sons," said Isis. "My country was granted good fortune in his time that she has not tasted before or since. His faith testifies to his truthfulness and piety. As for the sins committed during his revolution, there are always criminals who conceal themselves among the restless masses to launch their malicious acts of mayhem."

Osiris, after thinking for a moment, uttered his judgment: "Gentlemen, take your seats among the Immortals."

17

6

HORUS HAILED, "Amenemhat the First!"

A strongly built man of medium height entered, in the manner of those before him, until he stood before the throne.

Thoth, Scribe of the Gods, began reading aloud, "Leading ruler of the Middle Kingdom. He cleared the country of intruders, while putting a stop to internal quarrels. He presided over the provincial governors with wisdom, and he invaded the land of Nubia."

Osiris asked him to speak.

"I was one of the provincial potentates," said Amenemhat I, "when the central government was extremely weak and corrupt. The wars between the chiefs of the nomes did not abate until Bedouin tribes seized some parts of the realm. I was greatly saddened by what had befallen my country, and resolved to save her. Imposing austerity upon myself and my family, I drilled my men for action. Then I invaded the provinces surrounding me, and declared myself king, demanding the loyalty of the governors to me. In doing so, I was content to concede some prerogatives to them, while choosing my personal retinue from among their sons. Then I marched with a mighty army to rid the nation of the foreign interlopers. I set the administration in order, restoring the temples and spreading security and justice throughout the countryside. Following that, I struck into Nubia to set up a house of worship there to the gods that had backed my victory."

"You were nearly killed in a conspiracy among your courtiers," remarked Osiris. "How do you explain that?"

"A woman wanted to usurp the throne in favor of her son, and recruited some of the Nubians to help her."

"Nubia was a poor country, which could not endure the plunder of some of her lands to endow them for a temple," said Osiris.

"We encountered necessities that we could not avoid," Amenemhat I asserted.

"It was your duty to return power to the peasants," admonished Abnum. "But you forgot your own origins, and placed the edifice of the old oppressor back on its foundations, instead."

"The provincial governors had forgotten their roots, while putting the peasants back in power would have meant civil war!" Amenemhat I protested.

"You restored the sacred heritage of Egypt to her," said Khufu with approval.

Then Isis added, "He saved Egypt from chaos, and sat her once again on the throne of glory. He was unable to do more good than that."

"Take your place among the Immortals," pronounced Osiris.

7

HORUS SHOUTED, "Amenemhat the Second!"

Thoth then read aloud, "He followed his father's policies."

Summoned by Osiris to speak, Amenemhat II said, "I was thoroughly versed in all of my father's ways. Finding no better path, I followed them loyally and to the letter."

"But not to take a step forward is to take two steps backward," Abnum protested.

"I deepened Egypt's ties to Nubia," Amenemhat II rejoined. "And I forged new bonds with the land of Punt, from which we imported incense and perfumes."

Abnum asked a question of Osiris. "My Lord," he said, "shall all the Immortals be equal in the Other World?"

"You must learn, Abnum, that you are no longer a revolutionary," Osiris said dryly. "But there is no harm if I describe Destiny for you. Be aware that my trial sends souls to three different abodes: Paradise, the Inferno, and that which lies between the two, the Place of the Insignificant—for those who are not guilty, and merit neither Hell nor Heaven. In addition, there are distinct ranks in Heaven, among them kings and servants, according to the kind of work each performed in the world. . . ."

"For this king's sake," interrupted Isis, "take into account that the nation was blessed in his age with that which had graced his father's—safety and prosperity that could not be denied."

And so Osiris decreed, "Take your seat among the Immortals."

8

Horus called out, "Amenemhat the Third!"

A giant came in, walking in his winding sheet until he stood before the throne.

Thoth, Scribe of the Gods, then read aloud, "In his time, the state enjoyed stability, security, and strength. He directed his ardor to extracting minerals from the desert and revitalizing the means of irrigation. The harvests increased, and wealth spread over all."

Osiris asked him to speak.

"I inherited a stable kingdom," said Amenemhat III, "that I made even more secure by building a strong army. In my fifty-year reign, I fortunately was fated to send mining expeditions into the deserts. I reformed the methods for watering crops, and well-being overflowed from it. Literature and art rose as they never had before. In my epoch, the people used to chant and sing: *'He clothes the Two Lands in the garb of greenery; He is our nourishment—his mouth gives bounty.'*"

Osiris addressed him, "Your grandfather left a teaching that said:

> Summon all sternness to treat with those 'neath thee,
> For folk but revere those who fill them with fear.
> Make no one your brother and no one too dear!
> For who ate at my table rose up against me,
> And all whom I trusted came to betray me.

"So what did you reap from this?" he asked.

21

"I do not deny that it affected me greatly during the first part of my reign," answered Amenemhat III. "Every individual in my family was shaken by the conspiracy that nearly ended the life of my good and mighty grandfather—even those who were not yet born in his time. Some of my counselors urged me not to be clement with my subjects when they were rebellious or exceeded their proper bounds. Yet the heart does not hearken to a way of treating others except when it comes from an impulse within. I found that mine impelled me to love the people—I never hesitated to obey it, nor did I ever regret doing so."

"You were wrong, my son," said Amenemhat I. "Only your luck saved you from destruction."

"Yet you held true to the right and to good guidance," Ptahhotep commended him, "for when the heart speaks of goodness it is the God who has inspired it."

"How awful," exclaimed Abnum bitterly. "To speak well now of when the people were in power has become a subject of dispute!"

Isis then said, "This great and good son needs no defense for the portals of Paradise to open before him."

Osiris told him, "Go to your seat among the Immortals."

9

HORUS CALLED OUT, "Kings Sebekemsaf, Neferhotep, Si-Hathor, Neferkhera, Intef, and Timaios!"

The six entered in their shrouds and processed, bare of head and feet, until they stood before the throne.

Thoth then recited, "They each ruled for a short time. Each reign was known for its weakness, corruption, and internecine fighting over the throne, as well as the encroachments of the provincial governors and priests, the despotism of officials, and the hunger of the people. The thieves among nations fixed their eyes upon Egypt, until the Hyksos came to occupy her, and she suffered disgrace."

Osiris bid them to speak, and Sebekemsaf replied, "I lived under threat from my family and my courtiers, and was unable to confront the challenges that faced me."

The others spoke after him, saying much the same thing—then there was silence.

"Clearly," lamented Abnum, "there was not in all Egypt a man whose heart beat with sincerity. The state of the nation at this time was much like that which rallied the peasants to revolt in ours."

"All you think about is revolution," Amenemhat I upbraided him. "When I was governor of a nome, I found the country drowning in chaos. I did not therefore call for greater disorder, but trained my men and took over the throne, saving the land and the people, without violating our sacred customs, and without giving up either lives or honor."

"These men were feeble," Isis added, "and nothing can be done for the weak."

"You committed unforgivable crimes against the rights of your country," Osiris reproved the wretched sextet. "Weakness was not your only offense, for your hearts lacked nobility, and good intentions as well. Therefore, go to the Western Gate that leads unto Hell."

10

HORUS HERALDED, "King Seqenenra!"

A thin, tallish man came in, marching in his shroud until he stood before the throne.

Thoth, Scribe of the Gods, then recited, "He was Prince of Thebes, ruler of the Far South, the province that did not bow to the rule of the Hyksos—the so-called 'Shepherd Kings'—though he was compelled to pay them tribute. The Shepherds provoked him as they prepared to annex his domain to their immediate control, complaining that the lowing of the hippos in his palace's lake deprived their king's eyes of sleep. Yet he spurned the demand to surrender, leading his army to confront the foe. He had the good fortune to fall in battle, slain by numerous wounds to his head and face."

Osiris invited him to speak.

"I belong to the family that resisted the invasion," said Seqenenra, "fortifying ourselves in the South until the enemy tired of attacking us. A truce was proclaimed, leaving the South under my family's authority in return for an annual tax. This situation prevailed for over a hundred years, until I rose to the throne. I had spent no time thinking of the aggressor who had usurped our lands, nor had I prepared to combat him, when he seduced himself into creeping southward. My capacity in both men and matériel was limited, hence—while treating her as an equal—I annexed Nubia to my province, recruiting some of her men to strengthen my army. When the foe confronted me, opinions around me clashed: a minority called for defense of our

25

realm, while the majority warned of a terrible outcome. But I gave courage to the fearful while inciting their anxiety over religion, rule, and ideals until I aroused the defeatists to fight. My army fought doggedly, regaining some of its self-confidence by doing so. In one of the battles, the enemy encircled me, so I slew three of them, then spears and axes rained down upon me."

"Did you exhaust all political means before embarking on a futile war?" Ptahhotep asked.

"I did indeed," Seqenenra replied, "yet I would have needed three years more to prepare properly for the day of battle. But I later learned they had amassed their army even before they had sent me their warning."

"You lived as a hero," Abnum praised him, "and you died as a hero."

Isis said, "I repeat what my son Abnum said, that you lived as a hero, and died one too."

Osiris bid him, "Take your seat among the Immortals."

11

HORUS CALLED OUT, "King Kamose!"

A man of medium height and muscular build walked to his position before the throne.

Thoth, Recorder of the Divine Court, read aloud, "He took control on the same day in which his father was killed so that the will to fight was not lost, throwing himself without wavering into the fray. The war raged, sometimes in victory, sometimes in defeat, while he remained steadfast in command until he himself died."

Asked by Osiris to speak, Kamose recounted, "From the first moment, I found myself obliged to keep up the spirit of combat among my troops, shaken by the fall of their leader. I swooped down on the vanguard of the enemy, leaving not one of my soldiers a chance to balk. I never failed to appreciate my adversary's strength or superiority. For this reason, I chose as my redoubt a narrow place between the Nile and the mountain, taking up a defensive position until we could catch our breath and reassemble our forces. At the same time, I kept enlisting and training more and more men as well. Then I departed the world, having expended immense effort and vigilance."

"Both of us lived out our reigns in the field of battle," Menes said sympathetically.

"All kings are indebted to Egypt for their glory," mused Abnum, "except for this dynasty—to which Egypt is herself in debt."

"This monarch needs no defense from me," confessed Isis.

Osiris commanded Kamose, "Take your seat among the Immortals."

12

Horus hailed, "King Ahmose the First!"

A svelte man entered, walking in his winding sheet until he stood before the throne.

Thoth, Recorder of the Sacred Court, read aloud, "He took his father's place when the latter succumbed. He never flinched in fighting the foe, completing his preparations to shift from defense to attack. He affirmed a gift for leadership equal to his personal valor as he swept from victory to victory, besieging the Hyksos' capital at Avaris until he overcame it. Afterward, he hounded the enemy into Asia, where he chopped him up and scattered the pieces."

Osiris asked him to speak.

"In truth, I reaped the fruits of my family's long preparations," Ahmose I admitted, "and I was aided in my struggle by a son of the common people, the Commander Ahmose, son of Ebana. Each time that we won a battle, the warlike spirit rose in my men—as it fell among the forces of the enemy. From that point forward, we could not imagine that we would lose, while he could not imagine that he would win. With the fall of their city, the rule of the Hyksos came to an end, and Egypt again was free. My mind would not rest until we had driven them beyond our eastern borders, so that they could not reestablish themselves anywhere or contemplate revenge. I devoted the rest of my life to purging the land of their monuments and their appointees, in reorganizing the administration, and in reforming irrigation and the management of lands. When my era came to a close, Egypt was welcoming a new generation of her sons—resplendent with the courage of warriors, dreaming of foreign forays, and blazing with the spirit of martial expansion."

"Such a nature is new," remarked Khufu.

"And splendid, too," added Djoser.

"But perhaps not lacking in evil," cautioned Ptahhotep.

"Among such savages, there is no other path to an honorable life," said Seqenenra.

Isis interjected, "Then let us bless this son who has liberated our land."

Osiris told him, "Go to your seat among the Immortals."

13

HORUS HERALDED, "King Amenhotep the First!"

A stout, broad-shouldered man came in and stood humbly in his shroud before the throne.

Thoth then read from the book of the gods, "At the start of his reign, the Libyans crept into the west of the country. He threw them out after dealing them grievous losses, just as he expanded Egypt's southern borders, and invaded a wide swath of Syria."

Osiris invited him to speak, so he replied, "I took the throne with Egypt's past, both recent and distant, very much in mind. The elders had not forgotten the ghosts of the Hyksos and their humiliation of them, while the young reveled in the victories of Ahmose I and demanded to see more of such things. First, I strove to organize the administration by spreading the protection of the law and security and the proper supervision of those in the civil service. At that moment, the western borders were broached by the Libyans, to which I reacted swiftly. I exceeded the enemy's expectation and brought down upon him a shocking defeat. The fire of passion in the hearts of the commanders and officers set me aflame, so I undertook a successful attack in the unexplored regions of Nubia.

"Then my spies among the Hyksos informed me they were gathering with the ambition of gaining back what they had lost in our nation. So I set out at the head of a campaign and declared my rule over Palestine without having to engage in combat. I assailed the assembled Shepherds in the west of Syria, broke up their ranks, and destroyed the rest of what remained of them. I ordered the reconstruction of the temple of Amun, then returned the prisoners of war and captured livestock. I compelled the entire country to pay a head tax, and the nation's resources increased and the markets boomed."

"Everything you did was right," Ahmose I enthused, "for Egypt's southern borders are not secure without possessing Nubia, while the pivot of defense on our eastern borders lies in Syria."

"This means that Egypt's security was not truly established except by launching two different random aggressions outside our borders!" exclaimed the Sage Ptahhotep.

"I have learned that life is but a continuous conflict, in which the human being finds no rest," Ahmose I replied. "Whoever neglects to prepare his forces makes himself an easy prey to beasts who know nothing of mercy."

"I did not stint," said Amenhotep I, "on the most lavish of offerings in the temples to procure the blessings of the gods, for within their holy confines lies the first and last guarantee of Egypt's survival."

"This son's works are his testament," Isis opined.

"Go to your seat among the Immortals," ordered Osiris.

14

HORUS CALLED OUT, "King Thutmose the First!"

A lissome man of medium height advanced in his shroud until he stood before the throne.

Thoth read from the sacred scroll, "Domestic matters calmed during his reign. He undertook a military expedition to Nubia. He put down a revolt in Syria and extended his reach nearly to the borders of Naharin. He had wood imported from Lebanon, using it to build temples to the gods."

Osiris invited Thutmose I to address the court.

"My mother was a commoner," confessed Thutmose I, "thus my blood was not wholly royal. To make up for this, I married the Princess Ahmose, legitimizing my rule. My urge to see into the Unknown led me to invade Nubia in order to arrive at the sacred spring that lay at the source of the Nile. When I aimed my arrow at the enemy commander, he fell down dead—and I ripped his army to shreds. I was the first to reach the Third Cataract, where I erected five stelae to record our victories just as I built a fortress there as a garrison. I reorganized the administration, improving conditions for the tribes, and had almost returned to Thebes when news came to me of an uprising in Syria—which I put down by leading a campaign against it.

"Once back in Egypt, I decided to use the head tax exclusively for reform and construction, putting my trust in the genius of Ineni, who built two giant pylons at the entrance of the temple of Amun, as well as a great covered enclosure supported by columns made from the cedars of Lebanon. It was my good fortune to have restored the temple of Osiris—your own temple, My Lord—in the town of Abydos long since buried in sand, embellishing it with splendid furnishings and vessels of silver and gold, while creating religious endowments to maintain it as well."

"Why was there unrest in Syria?" asked Pharaoh Ahmose I.

"To put an end to the head tax," answered Thutmose I.

"Didn't you leave a garrison behind you, as you had done in Nubia?" queried Amenhotep I.

"No," came the reply, "I was wary of splitting my forces, but left behind a contingent to deal with emergencies."

"And thus we reap what we sow!" lamented the Sage Ptahhotep.

"You were humiliated to the point where you had to marry a princess in order to bestow legitimacy on your rule," bemoaned Abnum. "There's no shame in the fact that your mother was from the people. If only you had not disavowed the glorious popular revolution and its great rule, and drawn the veil of injustice over it, then you would not have subjected your dignity to this degradation."

"We blame you, O Divinity," Khufu inveighed against Osiris, referring to Abnum, "for bringing this strange agitator among us."

"He earned his place by meeting the obligation for divine and just rule," rebutted Osiris.

"This son is in need of no defense," declared Isis.

"To your place among the Immortals," Osiris ordered Thutmose I.

15

HORUS SHOUTED with his resounding voice, "King Thutmose the Second!"

A frail, emaciated man walked in and stood before the throne.

Thoth, Scribe of the Gods, read aloud, "He suppressed a rebellion that arose in the south, and another in Asia. Feeble and ailing, he was in power but a short time before departing to the other world."

Osiris asked Thutmose II to speak.

"When my father died," testified Thutmose II, "his sons all vied for the throne. Each one relied upon his own faction of followers. My father had put me forward for the succession, but my sister Hatshepsut seized it instead, marrying my brother to distract attention from her femininity. Although my faction could have restored my right by force, I took control without violence or bloodshed. Nor did I resort to revenge.

"Despite my poor health, I did not hesitate to suppress the revolt that sprang up in the south, and another in Asia, as well. Incapable of savoring life, I was unable to endure longer than a few years."

"You should have given up the throne in view of your weakness," Menes admonished him. "The weak should not aspire to rule."

"I triumphed anyway," retorted Thutmose II.

"Thanks to luck, and in spite of your frailty," Menes answered in scorn.

"He acted to the best of his ability," Isis declared. "I would compare his labor to that of the peasant who tills the land."

"Take your place among the Immortals," Osiris commanded Thutmose II.

16

Horus heralded, "Queen Hatshepsut!"

A full-figured woman of medium height came in. She walked in her winding sheet until she stood before the throne.

Thoth, Recorder of the Divine Court, read aloud, "Her reign passed in peace and prosperity. She erected the temple of Deir al-Bahari, and restored intercourse with the Land of Punt, whence she procured myrrh trees and their seedlings for the temple's grounds. Tribute rained down on her as she spread wealth everywhere, contenting the people."

Osiris asked her to speak.

"I was the only one worthy of the throne," Queen Hatsheput replied. "I was the last who remained in the line of Queen Ahmose and the divine royal blood, in contrast to my brother, Thutmose II, son of a morganatic wife named Mutnofret, and to my brother Thutmose III, whose mother was the concubine called Isis. Out of respect for an antiquated custom that rejects women's rule, I was forced to marry Thutmose III, who served as a priest in the Temple of Amun, and who—with the aid of the priests of that cult—never ceased scheming to put himself on the throne. Then the kingdom was wrenched from us as my brother Thutmose II took power with the support of his own party. When he died, rule returned to me, along with my brother Thutmose III. I imposed a wall of surveillance around him, to put an end to his machinations—and he crawled away into the shadows like a thing of no value. Meanwhile, I was helped by men such as Senenmut, Senmen, and Hapuseneb, who are considered among the greatest Egypt has known. I bestowed upon the masses a golden age of affluence and tranquility, until they came to believe that women are indeed capable of rule."

"In our time, which you have dismissed as an age of darkness, reigned two awesome queens," boasted Abnum.

"Why didn't you bolster your rule by sharing the throne with your brother?" wise Imhotep asked her.

"He was not, like me, of the sun god's lineage," she rejoined. "His interest was in weaving intrigues, and I had to be on guard from him. I was advised to have him murdered, but I detested treachery and the spilling of blood."

"Should it be understood from what you have said that the marital relations between you were merely official?" probed the Sage Ptahhotep.

"Yes," said Hatshepsut.

"Did you spend your life as a virgin?" he continued.

"You have no right to pose such a question, and the queen is free to disregard it," snapped Osiris.

Isis stepped in, "A daughter that would make any mother proud, and in need of no defense."

Osiris then directed, "Onto your seat among the Immortals."

17

HORUS HAILED, "King Thutmose the Third!"

A short, strongly built man, whose features projected majesty, entered the room wrapped in his shroud, then stood submissively before the throne.

"He took the throne at Hatshepsut's decease," read Horus, Scribe of the Gods, "purging the administration of his rivals, while seizing the reins of power with an iron grasp. He bestowed favor on the clergy of Amun, granting them primacy over all the priesthoods of the Two Lands. He mustered both an army and a fleet whose peers the nation had not known before, and boldly embarked on numerous wars, thereby creating the greatest empire that the ancient world had seen until his time. He annexed Asia Minor, the Upper Euphrates, the Mediterranean islands, the Western Desert oases, the highlands of Somalia, and the cataracts of the Upper Nile—making Egypt the crossroads for the races of all nations, the repository of traded goods and commodities. He built temples, forts, and obelisks, both within Egypt and in all the countries attached to her, leaving behind him a homeland perched at the summit of greatness and civilization."

Osiris invited Thutmose III to speak.

"At the start of my life, I tasted oppression as no king has known it," said Thutmose III. "Noting the strength with which the gods had endowed me, I was more deserving of rule than were my siblings. Yet though I acquired knowledge of the world, and of religion, I was denied my right because of a trifling technicality—my mother's origin as a commoner. I did not arrive at my right due to trickery, as some have said. Rather, the god Amun revealed me to his priests during his feast day. He stopped in front of me as I stood before the clergy, announcing his choice of me for the throne. I then prostrated myself before him in acceptance of his blessing.

"But the queen's faction set up a wall around me, and I dwelt in the shadows, like a man without the slightest weight. And so, when I seized the key positions of power after the death of the queen, I brought down the sternest chastisement on the men who had usurped my legitimate authority and sullied my marital bed. The woman's reign left only weakness as its legacy, for the army had fallen apart, while sedition spread through our foreign dominions as the prestige of Egypt and of her god Amun perished.

"The empire had been my greatest dream—not the love of killing, or the lust for wealth. Rather, I longed to spread the rays of Egyptian civilization, so that its radiance would shine over all the peoples around us, and Amun would occupy the highest place amongst all the gods."

"I witness that you achieved all of our dreams altogether," Ahmose I declared, "and acknowledge that you knew victory tens of times, but defeat not even once."

"What did you do for the peasants?" asked Abnum.

"My soldiers, officers, and commanders were drawn from them," Thutmose III replied. "I improved the methods of irrigation, took care of their needs, and exterminated the poverty in the places where they lived. I shifted a great many of them toward work in industries, crafts, and trade in the cities."

"You erected your empire," the Sage Ptahhotep upbraided him, "on the skulls of thousands upon thousands of Egyptians and others!"

"There is no avoiding death," rejoined Thutmose III. "Better a man die while building glory and good than wasting away in a plague or being bitten by a snake. In truth, I was not a tyrant, nor did I love the shedding of blood. I planned my wars based on thoroughness and surprise, to obtain the swiftest victory possible, with the least number of losses. After the siege of Megiddo, all of my enemies—soldiers, princes and kings—fell into my hands. They begged for mercy and my heart felt for them—so I let them live.

"I sent their sons to Thebes to learn science and civilization, to prepare them to rule their countries, rather than using Egyptian governors. This was a wise and humane policy not known before me."

"If it weren't for the riches that I left you," heckled Hatshepsut, "you would not have been able to launch a single campaign among the many you made in Asia."

"You did indeed leave me great wealth," conceded Thutmose III, "but you left the army in a mortal condition, and corruption was rampant among those closest to you."

"You are still a resentful, wrong-headed, and rotten person," protested Hatshepsut. "You remain determined to impugn my honor without any proof."

"I warn you not to exchange such wounding words," Osiris rebuked them.

"Did you love her, my son?" asked Isis.

"She used to mock my short stature —before which the kings of all nations would prostrate themselves abjectly."

"This great son is worthy," Isis lauded Thutmose III, "because he brought prestige to Egypt for many long ages."

"Go take your place among the Immortals," commanded Osiris.

18

HORUS BELLOWED, "King Amenhotep the Second!"

A gigantic man entered, inspiring awe with this height and broad build, marching in his shroud until he loomed before the throne.

"The throne has never known a man of his portly power," recited Thoth, Recorder of the Sacred Court. "His age was one of peace, as he devoted himself to building and public works."

Osiris asked Amenhotep II to speak.

"I was strong, so all those near me were afraid of me," he began. "I held them all to their duty, as though my eye followed their every move. I had a bow that only I could draw and shoot. Yet the well-established stability called for me to center my mission on building and construction—and so I did."

"What was your view regarding the grandeur of your forebears?" asked the Sage Ptahhotep.

"They were my highest example," answered Amenhotep II. "Yet I sometimes felt inadequate in comparison with them, and a great depression would seize me."

"In any case," said Isis, "you ruled and you built, while your times did not demand anything more than what you offered."

"Take your seat among the Immortals," Osiris told him.

19

Horus called out, "King Thutmose the Fourth!"

A tall, stringy man came in. As he stood before the throne, Thoth read from the holy scroll, "He came to power when the heir apparent died. A revolt broke out in the Asian territories, and he put the rebels down. He married Mutemwia, daughter of the king of Mitanni."

Osiris invited Thutmose IV to speak.

"I was not designated to take the throne," the king began. "One day, while visiting the Great Sphinx, I sat down in the shade of his paws. Something like drowsiness caressed me, and I heard the Sphinx's voice asking me to remove the sands from around him—and promising me the kingship if I did. Immediately, I called the workmen and ordered them to free him, assuming the entire responsibility for that myself. Then what had been predicted came to pass, as the heir apparent died, and I found myself on the throne without a rival.

"From the first day, I understood it was my duty to preserve the grandeur of our inheritance. So I punished the rebels and, in order to strengthen international ties, I married the daughter of Mitanni's king."

"Such a step looks like weakness to me," scolded Hatshepsut.

"I considered it a sensible policy," replied Thutmose IV.

"Choosing a queen from abroad is a matter fraught with peril!" interjected Khufu.

"I agree with the king that it was a very wise decision," opined the Sage Ptahhotep.

"Moreover," added Thutmose IV, "our royal harem has always included women from foreign nations."

"This man has done his duty, both at home and abroad," declared Isis.

"Proceed to your seat among the Immortals," Osiris bid him.

20

HORUS HERALDED, "King Amenhotep the Third and Queen Tiye!"

The royal couple came in, advancing in their shrouds until they halted before the throne.

Then Thoth, Scribe of the Gods, read aloud, "Queen Tiye was invited to rule alongside the king, whose era was one of such strength and prosperity as never had been seen before, while Egypt drank in the goods and wealth of the world. Meanwhile, Amenhotep III remained effectively vigilant over his empire. He put down any rebellion anywhere it arose, enjoying life as no pharaoh had done before him. He built palaces and temples, and displayed a fondness for food, drink, and women. In his final days, he married a daughter of the king of Mitanni who was the same age as his grandchildren, and who brought about his demise."

Osiris then invited the king to speak.

"I inherited the empire from my mighty grandfather, Thutmose III," said Amenhotep III, "and I was determined to inherit his greatness, as well. At that time there was no space for the empire to expand, so instead I reinforced its allies and crushed those who rose up against it. I displayed my greatness through a campaign of construction, and by providing material comfort to the masses. I defied tradition by marrying a woman from the common people: she was an outstanding partner for me in ruling the country, in the charm and wisdom that she brought to me. In the end, I left behind me an age that remains a byword for happiness and plenty."

"I was pleased by your testimonial to the queen's qualifications to rule," lauded Hatshepsut. "That is a witness to the competence of women as a whole, and an eloquent response to the attacks against them by their enemies."

"Tiye was a magnificent queen," agreed Amenhotep III, "according to the testimony of her enemies even before that of her friends."

"Yet you humiliated her in the most despicable way with your insatiable lust for other women," decried Abnum.

"Every king has his harem," Amenhotep III replied. "These fleeting passions did not diminish the great role of the queen."

"And you wed in your senility a woman the age of your grand-daughter?" continued Abnum.

"I wanted to strengthen the ties between Egypt and Mitanni," said Amenhotep III.

"Lies are forbidden in this sacred hall!" Osiris warned him.

"In truth," Amenhotep III answered apologetically, "I had heard of her unsurpassed beauty, and I was insane about this quality. Despite illness and old age, I overindulged in love until it undid me."

"Was this the acme of your long life's wisdom?" the Sage Ptahhotep needled him.

"Death by love is fairer by far than death by illness," said Amenhotep III.

X

Osiris asked Queen Tiye to speak.

"The king made me his wife out of love," she began. "I was drawn intensely to him, panting with passion and the splendor of Pharaoh. Love bound us together from then on always."

"One day he consulted me about some of his business as king, and my opinion deeply impressed him. 'You are a truly wise woman, as much as you are a much beloved female,' he told me."

"From that day forward, he never resolved an issue without first hearing my view, and we began to receive the ministers and other officials together. I employed my own personal vision in handling the business that came to our attention. Every high office holder in the kingdom acknowledged my ability and sagacity—the priests rushed to me for guidance when the religious crisis sparked by my son Akhenaten's creed grew out of control. I worked as hard I as could to avoid the catastrophe and prevent civil war.

"As for my husband's obsession with other women, all kings have their concubines. Not only is it not for a wife to plot her revenge on this score—it is also no shame for her to select his beauties for him, until he purges himself clean, restoring his sense of well-being. Through the force of my will as an exceptional woman, I triumphed, contenting myself that a queen is no ordinary female when responsible for her husband's policies."

"Was the queen never vanquished by the woman in you?" Hatshepsut put to her.

"I never knew defeat, except before my son."

"But a woman is still a woman," insisted Ptahhotep.

"Yet Tiye was of a kind never seen before—nor shall occur again," the queen replied.

"This lady has proven the worthiness of woman to rule even more than Hatshepsut herself had," advised Isis. "Her husband was a great king, and how preposterous that his appetite for women or taste for the pleasures of life in any way reduced his performance as pharaoh. Only after he had made his lowest subjects happy did he live a life of comfort and ease, in which they also shared with him. My heart is gladdened by this son and this daughter."

And so Osiris commanded them, "Go take your seats among the Immortals."

21

Horus hailed, "King Akhenaten and Queen Nefertiti!"

In came a man whose face fused both the male and the female, along with a ravishing woman. They walked forward in their winding sheets until they stood before the throne.

Thoth read from the divine tome, "Dual heirs to the throne and rule, they carried out their duties faithfully. A religious revolution dawned, calling for the worship of a new, sole deity. Abolishing the old gods, Akhenaten proclaimed the reign of love and peace, and the equality of human beings. Yet internally the country fell prey to dissent and corruption, while abroad the empire faced both dismemberment and loss. The land found itself on the verge of civil war, and the king fell from power. A counter-revolution then took hold: the historians and kings blotted his epoch from the annals, considering it the most destructive period ever for the country—one that destroyed it utterly."

Osiris bid Akhenaten to address the court.

"From a very early age," began Akhenaten, "I persistently sought to fill my soul with knowledge and divine wisdom, until the celestial inspiration descended into my heart—the light of the one and only God, and the call to worship him. I dedicated my life to that, then my rule, when I took the throne—in pursuit of the same goal. Immediately there arose a conflict between my luminous cause and the darknesses of ignorance and tradition, the ambitions of the priests and governors for higher rank and glory, the subjugation of the peasantry and the subjects of the empire. I never once resorted to violence in my holy spiritual struggle—I never approved the use of bloodshed or coercion. For some years, I tasted victory, and well-being spread its wings. But then the clouds of conspiracy and intrigue gathered, and the armies of darkness crept in around us, until they besieged us on all sides. I fell without any strength left, and defeat settled over me. Yet my trust in the final triumph never for a moment wavered. Never had a king known a life as heavenly as mine, nor an end so wretched."

"Believe what he has said, O Lord," Nefertiti beseeched Osiris. "We waged the struggle of heroes—until the forces of evil overwhelmed us. The looming tower was brought low, its foundations fallen in."

The first to comment was the wise Imhotep. "We had always surmised that the power of the one Deity lay behind Amun, Ra, Ptah, and the pantheon of gods," he said. "But we observed that the people clung to their bodily images, gathering around them in every province to gain strength and solace, so we let things continue as they were. This was a mercy to believing hearts, saving them from oblivion."

"We found the people lost in error," rejoined Akhenaten. "The time had come for them to face the Truth, in all its aspects."

"Handling the people is a difficult art, Your Highness," answered Ptahhotep. "He who does not master it will find his benevolent impulses frustrated, and will kill what he loves while striving to save it."

"If it weren't for those seeking personal interest," complained Akhenaten, "we could have achieved the salvation of those we love."

"What did you do with those who opposed you for selfish motives?" asked Abnum.

"I committed myself from the beginning," answered Akhenaten, "to treat others with kindness, to avoid harm and aggression."

"Evildoers deserve naught but the club and the sword!" exclaimed Abnum.

"I believed in love for one's enemies, as well as one's friends."

"Your message was lost through your own naivete," Abnum upbraided him. "The only good man is a warrior!"

"I left for you the greatest empire in history," added Thutmose III. "How could it have perished when you such had an incomparable army waiting at your command?"

"Love and peace were my ideals," replied Akhenaten.

"Please go on," Osiris urged him.

"I preached for the One God, who is the Father and the Mother to all humanity," Akhenaten continued. "They are all equal under His shelter. I used to call for love to replace the sword in the relations between people."

"No wonder the empire was lost with this kind of thinking," Thutmose III reproved him. "You must be crazy!"

"I will not permit anyone's speech to cross the bounds of courtesy," Osiris rebuked him. "Apologize!"

"I apologize," Thutmose III replied, "but I also declare my regret that my life was spent in vain!"

"I unified Egypt with the sword," Menes reminded Akhenaten, "on a hill of skulls. By necessity, the empire was created by the same means. Yet to our misfortune, an enemy called 'ideas' inflicted itself upon us, invading us from within—and turned our glory into a laughingstock."

"Your debate is pointless," Akhenaten replied dismissively. "The matter, pure and simple, is that I heard the voice of the God. And that this heavenly blessing did not descend on you."

"Always we were pursued by these same views, both from our enemies and our friends," remarked Nefertiti. "The world shattered us with its brutality, but today we stand here before a just divinity."

"Then why did you abandon your husband when the crisis reached its climax?" Hatshepsut confronted her.

"I never doubted him," Nefertiti answered defiantly. "But I was deluded to think that if I left him, I could save him from being killed."

"This son was entrusted with a message by which he strove to save mankind," Isis said to them. "Yet no one was ready either to understand him, or to reach an accord with him—and this was the tragedy. I shall remain proud of him for all eternity."

"Take your seat, with your wife, among the Immortals," Osiris told him.

22

HORUS HAILED the court, "King Smenkhkara, King Tutankhamun, and King Aya."

Thoth, the Sacred Recorder, read aloud, "Smenkhkara ruled for four years, Tutankhamun for six years, and Aya for four years. Their reigns were times of disturbance and corruption. None of them was capable of confronting the crisis."

Osiris asked them to speak.

"I began my rule as coregent with Tutankhamun," responded Smenkhkara, "but I was not able to restore the throne's prestige."

"Real authority lay with the priests of Amun," said Tutankhamun.

"And the influence of the priests increased in my time," admitted Aya. "I was weakened by age, and failed to achieve reform."

"How could you repudiate me," Akhenaten grilled Aya, "when you were the closest person to me, and I was your wife's father?"

"I renounced you to avoid civil war in our country," answered Aya.

"You were unfaithful to the One True God after you had proclaimed your belief in Him right in front of me."

"My three sons were not suited for the throne," Isis asserted. "Without the blind law of hereditary succession, not one of them would have sat on the throne, yet they deserve mercy, just the same."

Osiris turned to them.

"Go to the Northern Gate," he bid them, "which leads to the Realm of Purgatory."

23

HORUS CALLED OUT, "King Horemheb!"

A brawny, stern-faced man of middling stature came in, walking in his winding sheet until he stood before the throne.

Thoth, Scribe of the Gods, then read aloud, "He came to power though not from the royal line. So, despite her advanced age, he married Mutnodjmet in order to legitimize his rule. By main force he ended the chaos, corruption, and neglect, while repairing the damage to the temples after Akhenaten. Thanks to him, security and order were established inside the country. As for the empire, by that time it already—except for a small portion—belonged to the past."

Osiris then invited Horemheb to speak.

"True, I was not of royal blood, yet I came from a venerable old family in the north of Egypt. My upbringing was military, and I rendered many successful services to Pharaoh Amenhotep III. When Akhenaten took the throne, he brought me close to him, bestowing his confidence upon me. Yet to my great regret, he did not take my advice and impose the necessary punishments for corruption within the country and dispatch expeditions to put down the rebels throughout the empire. When the crisis worsened, and the first warnings of civil war loomed on the horizon, I reached an understanding with the priests of Amun to put an end completely to Akhenaten's rule. Everyone agreed that I had the competence to confront the anarchy that then prevailed all over Egypt. Yet it was also necessary to uphold legality, so first Smenkhkara, then Tutankhamun, and finally

Aya became kings in succession. When Aya passed away, a revolution erupted—the tombs were plundered, and I found no escape from the obligations of loyalty. So I married Mutnodjmet, the sister of Nefertiti, for she was among the first to repent of Akhenaten's heresy, and who agreed to join with the priests of Amun in order to save the country. I found before me a heavy and many-sided mission, but I lacked neither in strength nor determination. I smothered the revolt, and organized anew the army, police, and administration. I kept an eye on the civil servants, and showed no mercy to the corrupt among them. Next I restored the places of worship and the religious estates, defending the weak against the strong. And if I had been granted a longer life, I would have regained what had been lost of the magnificent empire of Thutmose III."

"You did a glorious job, O king!" Khufu praised him.

"A glorious job indeed," Abnum snapped sarcastically. "No one can blame you for not returning the power to the people, since you are from such a well-rooted family. My frank translation of that is a family well-rooted in looting and plunder!"

"I do not approve of your manner of speaking—apologize!" said Osiris imperiously.

"I apologize," mumbled Abnum.

"You were the right man to return the empire to its glory of old," said Thutmose III.

"The land was torn apart and in a state of moral ruin," Horemheb answered him. "The chaos was beyond anyone's imagining."

"I loved none of my followers more than you, Horemheb," Akhenaten reproached him. "Nor was I as generous with anyone as much as I was with you. My reward was that you betrayed me, making alliance with the enemies of the people as well as my own. Then you tore down my temple as well as my city. You scratched out my name and poured out curses upon me."

"I deny nothing you have said," replied Horemheb. "I loved you more than any man I'd ever known—but I loved Egypt more."

"You helped blot out the adoration of the One and Only God," seethed Nefertiti, "to hoist the host of imposters back on their thrones."

"I say to the queen in this hall, in which no lie is permitted, that no woman ever occupied my heart except to the smallest extent possible," declared Horemheb. "My battle with you both was purely a patriotic one, not at all one of romantic intrigue!"

"This son is too powerful to need any defense!" exclaimed the goddess Isis.

"Take your seat among the Immortals," Osiris commanded him.

24

Horus heralded, "King Ramesses the First!"

A tall, elderly man entered, advancing in his shroud until he stopped before the throne.

Thoth, Recorder of the Divine Court, recited to those present, "He was already old when he began his rule. He started to build a many-pillared hall in the temple of Karnak, but expired before he could finish it."

Osiris called upon Ramesses I to speak.

"When Horemheb died, he left no legitimate heir to the throne of Egypt," commenced Ramesses I. "At that time, I was a lector-priest in the temple of Amun, known for my wisdom and correctness of opinion, as well as for my piety. Hence the God chose me to sit on the throne. The empire was never out of my thoughts, but the condition of the country did not allow me to embark on a lengthy war. So I ordered the proper care for the land and for the means of irrigation in order to boost the wealth of the nation. And I launched the construction of the hypostyle hall—yet I did not have enough time to see it completed."

"Perhaps the selection of this king was not propitious," cautioned Isis, "but at that moment, Egypt did not have the right man at hand. As for this man, he tried as hard as he possibly could, and he bears no blame for his situation."

Osiris turned to him, "Go to your place among the Immortals."

25

Next Horus called out, "King Seti the First!"

In came a man tall of stature and powerfully built. He walked, wrapped in his winding sheet, until he stood before the throne.

Then Thoth, Scribe of the Gods, read aloud, "He assumed the throne upon the death of his father. He subdued Nubia, returned Palestine to Egypt, then focused his energies on building and construction."

Following this, Osiris invited Seti I to speak.

"From the first day I strove to follow a well-laid plan," Seti I said. "This was to shore up authority at home, while marching southward to our furthest borders, then taking Palestine back by victory over the Hittites, sealed by a pact of peace. This done, I completed the many-pillared hall at Karnak and restored the temples that had not before known a repairing hand. Throughout my reign security, order, and justice fared well, while ease and opulence overspread the land. The arts and literature flourished. The good life ruled, though near the end a conflict arose between my heir apparent and his brother."

Thutmose III asked him, "Why didn't you continue to combat the Hittites?"

"I felt that my army was exhausted," Seti I replied, "while at the same time the Hittites as a nation were extremely tough in battle."

"The only glorious way to deal with an enemy," Thutmose III retorted, "is to fight against him, not to make a treaty of peace with him!"

"A treaty of peace is preferable to a war without glory," Seti I answered.

At this, Akhenaten inquired, "Why did you not apply the Divine Law, the law of love and peace?"

Horemheb cut in sharply, "That which led to the empire's ruin and left it defenseless?"

"Did you join yourself to the Divine Lineage," Khufu queried, "in order to rule as a son of the gods?"

"I did this with my wife at the temple of Amun, in accordance with the observed rituals," Seti I told him.

"I am pleased with this son, so lofty of purpose!" Isis exclaimed.

And so Osiris pronounced judgment, "Come take your place among the Immortals."

26

AGAIN, HORUS HERALDED, "King Ramesses the Second!"

Then entered a tall, fit-looking man who advanced in his shroud until he loomed before the throne.

Thoth, Recorder of the Divine Court, declaimed, "He came to the throne at his father's demise. He buttressed Egypt's rule over Nubia and Asia. He waged war against the Hittites, then concluded with them a treaty of peace. Thenceforth he devoted the rest of his long life to a campaign of construction of a kind never before seen in the history of his country. It was an age of building and of a blossoming of the arts, and of luxury. His life stretched to nearly a century, and he enjoyed it to the full, siring nearly three hundred children."

Then Osiris asked him to speak.

"In truth, I usurped the throne from my brother, the heir apparent," Ramesses II replied. "I was certain that the hour demanded a man of power, while my brother's weakness, despite his legitimate claim to rule, would bring disaster to Egypt. I was boldly ambitious, determined to provide the greatest degree of security, order, justice, and prosperity to my country at home, while bringing back to our empire its splendor of old. I deepened our dominion over Nubia, then did the same in Palestine, Syria, and the Lebanon, whose rulers and princes rushed forward to swear their oath of submission.

"Next I turned toward Qadesh to deliver the decisive blow to my strongest adversary, the king of the Hittites. But to my bad luck I found myself encircled by the foe, while the rest of my forces were quite far from me, in the south. I felt a rage rising within me, out of fear for Egypt's honor, which I held within my own hands. I prayed a long time to my God, reminding Him that I had only left my country to raise up His name and to impose His majesty. Then I fell upon the enemy, with the pick of my personal guard around me. I smote them like a thunderbolt. As the light of my glory shattered their hearts and their doom came inexorably under my blows, I drove a gap between them and passed through it to reach my army. Then we wheeled back around at them and beat them down until they threw themselves into the river, and our victory was complete.

"Following this I laid siege to Qadesh, suggesting an armistice to the king. I did not find this shameful, as I had regained territories for the empire that had not previously been restored. Afterward I dedicated my life to construction, marrying the daughter of the Hittite monarch as a way of cementing our peace. I erected structures of sorts never before built by any pharaoh. I brought forth happiness to the people of Egypt such as they had not known until then, and which I doubt they have known since."

"Yet you began your career by usurping your brother's right as to the throne," his father, Seti I, scolded him.

"I cannot respect a law which would grant the throne to a feeble man who does not deserve it."

"Where did you get your power to know the Divine Will?" Akhenaten taunted him. "What you have said about your brother was said about me, yet I was the first ruler to create a kingdom for the One True God on earth."

"But that was a catastrophe for both the nation and the empire. . . ." Ramesses II rejoined.

Thutmose III then asked, "Pray tell me how it behooved a triumphant leader like yourself not only to make a treaty of peace with your enemy, but to marry his daughter, as well?"

"He was the one who asked for it," said Ramesses II, "and I found it beneficial to both parties."

"And how, O King, did you find yourself surrounded in battle?" continued Thutmose III.

"Two of the enemy's spies fell into our hands. They falsely informed us that the Hittite army was to the north of Qadesh," answered Ramesses II. "I thus hurried with the vanguard of my troops to take the land south of the city. However, the enemy was actually lying in wait to the east, from which he struck to encircle me."

"You set off in haste when you should have waited for your army to reach you from the south," said Thutmose III. "You are courageous—there is no doubt about that—but you are not a prudent commander."

"Yet I broke through the siege, then turned the attack back on the enemy with the rest of my army," Ramesses II protested. "They then fell into the trap which they themselves had set for me—I tore them to pieces and scored a decisive victory."

"Your objective was not merely to win a battle," Thutmose III said, moving to the point of his discourse. "Rather, you clearly wanted to conquer Qadesh, as I had done, because it controls the roads in every direction. Therefore, you have no right to claim victory when you did not achieve the purpose of your expedition."

"What do you say about my routing the enemy's army?" Ramesses II asked.

"I say that you won a battle but you lost the war," Thutmose III riposted, "while your enemy lost a battle but won the war. He enticed you to make peace in order to reorganize his ranks. He welcomed your relationship by marriage in order to fix your friendly attitude before making good his losses. He was content to keep Qadesh as a place from which to threaten any point in your empire in future."

"During all of my long reign, the security of my homeland was not disturbed for even one hour," Ramesses II responded. "Nor was there a single violent rebellion anywhere in our vast empire, while no enemy dared cast an aggressive glance at our borders."

"I cannot dismiss your merit," Thutmose III conceded. "You restored to Egypt the greatest part of her empire, and were marked by your overwhelming personal valor, which put fear into the hearts of your enemies."

"And do not forget that my era was the greatest age of construction in the country," said Ramesses II.

"Did you build a pyramid?" Khufu asked him.

"No, but man does not build pyramids alone," said Ramesses II. "There is not one province in Egypt without a temple or an obelisk or a statue of mine."

"But you appropriated my ruined temple and turned it into your own funerary complex," Akhenaten intervened. "You repeated this assault on your other predecessors' monuments, engraving your name where it did not rightfully belong. You minimized the accomplishments of all the great ones who came before you, as if the One God had created only you alone."

"In this sacred hall I will not deny any error or defend any impetuous act," Ramesses II retorted, "but I would prefer that someone innocent of heresy and licentiousness accuse me."

Osiris broke in, "Don't forget, O King, that you are addressing someone who has endured this same trial and emerged from it as an Immortal. Apologize."

Ramesses II muttered, "I apologize."

"What of your experience with women?" Queen Hatshepsut queried him. "And did you find time to treat kindly with your three hundred children?"

"No man has savored happiness such as I did," Ramesses II replied. "The gods endowed me with long life, perfect health, and limitless powers for love. These remained undiminished until the end, despite all the affection that my wife, Queen Nefertari lavished upon me. As for my children, I never knew more than a few of them."

"Did you use magic to preserve your marvelous manly vigor?" Amenhotep III inquired.

"I performed my own magic myself," Ramesses II explained. "At the age of ninety, I would stand in the Great Hall while rows of chariots entered. In each rode one of my wives, naked, accompanied by a naked slave girl. They would keep rolling past me until there flowed in my aged veins the fresh blood of youth!"

"Were these the same chariots with which you scored your military victories?" the Sage Ptahhotep wondered.

"No," Ramesses II said. "These were the chariots of love, clad with pure gold, exuding the sumptuous aromas of women."

"Your life, O King, mixed both seriousness in all its senses, and play with all its caprices," jibed Abnum. "Perhaps the final judgment upon you should combine both indulgence and restraint!"

Osiris stared at Abnum sternly. "This proceeding has no need either for your guidance or your opinions, except to ignite a new revolution in the world of Eternity," he berated him. "Do not exceed your proper place—apologize!"

Abnum acquiesced, "I beg your pardon, Great Lord!"

Isis summarized, "This son returned Egypt to her former glory, while material comfort during his time spread from palace to house to reed hut alike. If we counted all his faults through all of his life, they would seem insignificant."

And so Osiris turned to Ramesses II, "Go take your seat among the Immortals."

27

Horus called out, "King Merneptah!"

A tall man of middling years came in, marching with his familiar bearing until he took his place before the throne.

Thoth, Recorder of the Divine Court, then read aloud, "He expended his entire ten years of rule in defense of the empire, and did no wrong to anyone."

Osiris invited him to speak.

"My father lived so long that he did not leave any of his sons even the least hope of assuming the throne," recounted Merneptah. "Dozens of my siblings died between youth and middle age, until I became the designated heir—then the ruler at age sixty. When the great king vanished, the chieftains of sedition began to stir—so I got up to sling my sword, despite my advanced age. I overcame the upstarts in Asia and totally destroyed an invasion from the West. I took hold of the country's reins with a firm hand in domestic affairs, and as peace spread at home, security prevailed."

"You attacked older monuments to erect palaces and temples," remarked Akhenaten, "engraving upon them the story of your father's deeds!"

"All my time was absorbed in warfare—I never had time to do any building," Merneptah replied.

"I can say you are a brilliant commander," said Thutmose III.

"Thank you, my son," Isis addressed Merenptah, "for your heroism and sincerity."

Osiris ordered him, "Go to your place among the Immortals."

28

HORUS HERALDED, "King Amenmessu, King Siptah, and King Seti the Second!"

The three walked in, wrapped in their winding sheets, until they stood before the throne.

Thoth, the sacred scribe, recited from their record, "They were all preoccupied with contending for the throne. Corruption reigned supreme, as greed rent the unity of the country asunder, and killing, looting, and plunder ran rampant in the land."

Osiris called upon them to speak, and Amenmessu was the first to respond. "I took the throne by right. Yet I was surrounded by conspiracies, and fell after only one year."

"I was entitled to rule," asserted Siptah, "but it was usurped from me in a dispute that arose between myself and Merneptah near the end of his reign. I was distracted from my duties in chasing down malicious plots, until I was forced to give up the throne."

"I strove to the limits of my strength to be a good ruler," insisted Seti II. "But the corruption worsened, and the general putrefaction swept us away."

"How quickly corruption replaces virtue," lamented the Sage Imhotep, vizier to King Djoser. "See how the weakness of a single ruler is reflected back onto an entire civilization!"

"Perhaps the problem in the end is," Thutmose III suggested, "how to find the right, powerful man at the right time?"

"There wasn't any man in the royal family who was powerful enough," countered Horemheb. "Yet could it be that there was no such man to be found in the land?"

"The law demands that the heir who is present be granted the throne," said Isis, "not to suffer the difficulties of finding someone else who has the right qualities. These three could only do what they were able to do."

"Get all ye to Purgatory," said Osiris imperiously.

29

HORUS CALLED OUT, "Pharaoh Sethnakht!"

A short, strongly built man entered, covered in his shroud, then strode with dignity to his place before the throne.

Then Thoth read from his holy tome, "He restored the law to its sovereignty!"

Osiris invited him to speak, so he began, "I lived in an age of chaos. I was nearly murdered one day as I sailed on the Nile —and survived by a miracle. I was then but a distant relative of the King Merneptah, but rose to the throne with the aid of the priests. The corrupt provincial governors refused to acknowledge me. While not powerful enough to subjugate them all, I was not lacking in courage. So I crushed the nome of Khnum, where I annihilated the rebels, cutting off the ears and noses of those I captured. From there I marched on Thebes, where the cowards quickly rushed to greet me in submission.

"I put right the army and the forces of order, and labored tirelessly until I returned the law to its place of supremacy. I made the farmer safe on his land, and once again he tilled the soil. But I departed the world before I could make the peoples of our empire feel the might of Egypt once more."

"Your work, that but a few words could describe, was greater than the building of the Great Pyramid," marveled Khufu.

"My heart has begun to beat again," chimed Menes.

"A magnificent son, who has hewn his indomitable will in souls, not in stone," lauded Isis.

Osiris bid him, "Proceed to your seat among the Immortals."

30

HORUS HERALDED, "King Ramesses the Third!"

A lumbering giant of a man came in, and moved in his winding sheet till he loomed before the throne.

Thoth, Recorder of the Sacred Court, then read aloud, "He was victorious over invaders from Asia and the West, and over the Sea Peoples too. The nation dwelt in peace and protection."

Osiris asked him to address the proceedings.

"Due to the unrest inside Egypt, the Levantine rulers threw off their traces. Meanwhile, the Libyans lusted to conquer our land. Then suddenly we were flooded on our northern coast by peoples coming with their whole families, who set up colonies inside the country. In the event, I launched into ruthless combat, driving the Libyans from our soil. I exterminated the Sea Peoples, making captives of their women and young. Next I commanded a campaign in Asia, decimating them without mercy. During my time, Egypt was graced with security and stability, as I erected multitudes of palaces and temples.

"But from sheer bad fortune, in my old age, a conspiracy hatched in my harem aimed to seize the throne by force. I created a tribunal to try those responsible, and ordered that justice be served, with no criminal acquitted and no innocent condemned. Yet tragically, two of the judges succumbed to the allure of the women accused, and took their own lives when their lapse was exposed."

"Your record reveals you are a most extraordinary leader," said Thutmose III.

"I followed your footsteps in my conquest of Asia," replied Ramesses III.

"Your treatment of the conspirators is to your credit," added Akhenaten. "Your putting them forward for trial rather than striking them down on the spot, your prompt setting up of the court in order to carry out an investigation to arrive at justice—all this bears witness to your reverence for the law, and your passion for the noble deeds of morality. It's as though you were among the worshipers of the One and Only God."

"I too adored the noble deeds of morality, which is how all the believers of the gods were raised."

"The wiles of women nearly killed a great king," tut-tutted the Sage Ptahhotep, "while causing the deaths of two judges, as well."

"The One God fashioned women to expose the elements that men are made of," said Queen Nefertiti. "The precious and the worthless, too!"

"Welcome to this son, who is both great and noble in one!" exclaimed the goddess Isis.

"Go to your place among the Immortals," pronounced Osiris.

31

Horus heralded, "The kings Ramesses IV, V, VI, VII, VIII, IX, X, XI, and XII."

Nine men of varying shapes and sizes came in, wrapped in their winding sheets, and walked in a row until they stood before the throne.

Thoth, Scribe of the Gods, recited from the book before him, "They each ruled for a short time only, one after the other, and none cared for anything but to hang onto power. They let their lusts run away with them—and things fell apart. Wickedness was rampant, the area of the north coast seceding under the last of their line."

Osiris bid them to speak—but they all remained silent.

Ramesses II then asked them, "Why did you take my name as your own? Are we related in any way?"

"We took it in order to be blessed and ennobled!" said Ramesses IV.

"But you had none of my fortitude, and, in truth, you did not live up to it," retorted Ramesses II.

"I cannot request their forgiveness," said Isis, "but I do ask for mercy."

"To Purgatory with the lot of you," commanded Osiris.

32

HORUS BELLOWED, "The governor Nesubenedbed!"

A stout man of medium height stepped in, striding forward until he stood before the throne.

Thoth, the Divine Record Keeper, then read aloud, "As viceroy of the northern region, he broke away from Egypt during the reign of Ramesses XII. The malaise within the country was matched by the fading of her influence abroad."

Osiris asked him to speak, so Nesubenedbed began, "I sprang from the elite of Tanis, and it distressed me to see Egypt fall into chaos and disunity. I was not able to seize the throne, so I declared the independence of the northern area, hoping to establish order and security there. To this end, I devoted the utmost energy."

"I am the one most qualified here to interpret the speech of those born to privilege," boasted Abnum. "Though they always call for security and welfare, they only want those things for themselves, at the expense of the peasants and the dispossessed."

"The oneness of our homeland, to which I dedicated my whole life, was ended by your actions," moaned Menes.

"I deplore the blindness of those who surrounded you," added Ptahhotep.

"I do not know how to defend this son," admitted Isis.

"To the gates of Hell," fumed Osiris.

33

OSIRIS MOTIONED TO THOTH, who duly recited, "The will of the gods decreed that Libya should attack Egypt, becoming its ruling dynasty. Near the end of their rule, Egypt was rent into many parts, the provinces divided one from another, and things returned to how they had been before the age of Menes.

"Then the Assyrians invaded in turn, as the sorrows continued to mount."

34

HORUS HERALDED, "King Psamtek the First!"

A boney, bent-over man came in, walking in his shroud until he stood before the throne.

Thoth, Recorder of the Divine Court, then read aloud, "He proclaimed himself monarch over Egypt. He brought back the nation's unity and fixed the foundations of order. He marshaled a mighty army made up of foreign mercenaries, using it to reimpose Egypt's dominion over Palestine."

Osiris summoned him to speak.

"I was a descendant of Sethnakht," said Psamtek I, "one of twelve princes who governed in the northern province in the shadow of the Assyrians. Due to foreign factors, the power of the Assyrians began to wane, so I resolved to declare Egypt's independence and territorial integrity. I ended the authority of the princes through a series of assaults, announcing myself as Egypt's pharaoh. I appointed my sister Nitocris as high priestess of Thebes in order to assert my hold on the clergy, and the nation's union and internal disciple were restored.

"I concentrated on the economy, while recruiting an army of Greeks and Carians, as well as Syrians and Libyans. The people were blessed with security and prosperity, and harked back on their own to the Old Kingdom in taste, tradition, and the rituals of worship—I saw no harm in that. Egypt's sovereignty over Palestine returned, and the country became again nearly what it was five hundred years before, under Ramesses III.

"A majestic achievement, for which we are grateful," said the wise Imhotep, vizier to King Djoser.

"What could be more beautiful than for a people to revive their ancient heritage," Khufu agreed.

"I consider it a reactionary movement—how do you interpret it, King Psamtek?" asked Akhenaten.

"The people suffered such humiliation under the foreigners that they launched a peaceful revolution against their imported customs—seeking refuge in their original roots and their ancestral traditions."

"But you yourself marched in an opposite direction," noted Thutmose III, "and put up an army of alien troops!"

"Egypt was threatened from the east, west, and south," explained Psamtek I, "but the Egyptians had lost their military drive, and were resigned to defeat. I saved the situation with the means available."

"See what he has done for his homeland," rhapsodized Isis, "under the most arduous conditions possible!"

"Take your seat among the Immortals," decreed Osiris.

35

HORUS CALLED OUT, "Pharaoh Nekau the Second!"

A tall, amply fleshed man walked in, wrapped in his shroud, and stood before the throne.

Thoth, Scribe of the Gods, then read aloud, "He extended his rule unto Syria, and was victorious over Assyria and Judah. But Babylon was rising at the same time, and conquered Syria and Palestine as well. He strengthened the forts along the border and sought to improve trade, even sending an expedition of Phoenicians to explore the far shores of Africa."

Osiris bid him speak.

"I never, ever neglected my duty," said Nekau II simply. "I met with luck at my life's beginning, and with defeats at its ending. But the homeland enjoyed soundness, security, well-being during my rule."

"You must have realized," Thutmose III reminded him, "that young nations have no limits to their ambitions. You had to ready the people to fight!"

"Tragically, the people had lost their spirit," Nekau II admitted mournfully.

"You too had lost your spirit," the Sage Ptahhotep berated him, "for you put your faith in foreign hirelings!"

"He never flagged in the struggle," said Isis, "either on the field of battle, or on our fertile soil."

"Take your seat among the Immortals," Osiris told him.

36

HORUS HERALDED, "King Psamtek the Second!"

A short, plump man entered the chamber, waddling in his winding sheet until he stood before the throne.

Thoth, Recorder of the Divine Court, then recited, "He strengthened order at home, and to that end, made his daughter, Enekhnes-Neferibre, High Priestess of Amun, in place of her paternal aunt, Nitocris. And he deepened his relations with Greece."

Osiris asked him to speak.

"I have nothing to add," said Psamtek II, "save that my reign was one of peace and clemency."

"You forgot," Thutmose III reproached him, "that Egypt was once an empire!"

"What's the use of dwelling upon youth that has passed?" answered Psamtek II.

"And you forgot that Babylon lay in wait at the frontier?" King Ahmose I demanded.

"And what did you do to instill the love of combat among the populace?" asked King Ahmose I.

When he did not reply, Isis inserted, "His era was a time of wealth and tranquility!"

"Get thee to Purgatory," bade him Osiris.

37

HORUS CALLED OUT, "King Apries!"

A stocky man stalked in, wrapped in his shroud, and stopped before the throne.

Thoth the Divine Recorder read aloud, "He incited Israel against Babylon, taking part in the fighting by invading Phoenicia with his navy—but was met with a total rout. Prince Ahmose II broke his pledge of obedience to him, and in the struggle that followed King Apries was killed."

Asked by Osiris to speak, Apries explained, "Babylonia was my greatest worry. The centerpiece of my plan was to goad Israel to attack Babylon. My part was to penetrate Phoenicia with my fleet in order to outflank the enemy—but the gambit failed, and I was utterly defeated instead."

"The plan could not be faulted," Thutmose III said, "but to succeed it needed able hands."

"I beg you to show him mercy," pleaded Isis.

"Off with thee to Purgatory," Osiris told Apries.

38

HORUS HERALDED, "King Ahmose the Second!"

A tall, gaunt man stepped into the room. He paced to his place facing Osiris on his throne.

Thoth, Scribe of the Gods, then recited, "He bolstered the domestic order of the country. He relied excessively on an alliance with the Greeks, and overly indulged in dinners with wild drinking. During his reign, Persia emerged as a great power. To restrain her, Ahmose II sought to align Egypt with Babylonia and Greece, but Babylonia was destroyed."

When Osiris invited him to speak, Ahmose II explained, "I considered King Apries responsible for his defeat before Babylon and that he was too weak to face the complex situation that confronted him. Thus I broke my pact with him and assumed the throne in his place. Then I fashioned an alliance to block the Persians, but the Persians won. Thereafter I turned to internal reform."

"What did you do in domestic affairs?" Queen Hatshepsut queried.

"The country was notably affluent under me. And I enhanced civil law—it is enough to cite the rule requiring the rich to declare the sources of their wealth to the mayor of their city."

"How did you prepare the common folk to deal with the nouveaux riches?" asked Thutmose III.

"My people were only concerned with farming and their own private lives," said Ahmose II.

"You served as their example, in your love of riotous feasting with wine," jibed Ramesses II. "I have nothing against such banquets— if the one who gives them is great!"

"His excellent works are not inconsiderable," Isis interjected. "His plan was a wise one, though it failed."

Osiris thought for a while, then pronounced, "You shall languish in Purgatory for a thousand years, before dwelling in the particular level of Paradise appropriate to your modest merit."

39

HORUS RAISED HIS VOICE to extol, "King Psamtek the Third!"

A strongly built man of medium height advanced in his winding sheet until he stood before the throne.

Thoth commenced to read from the sacred tome before him, "He reigned for three months. Then he and his army defended Egypt against the Persian king, Cambyses, but his forces were routed and he fell captive to the foe. Cambyses slew him and seized control of the country."

Osiris asked him to address the court.

"I came to the throne as the Persian armies were penetrating Egypt," replied Psamtek III, "so I prepared my Greek troops for battle while urgently conscripting a small army of Egyptians. I met the enemy in a fierce engagement, but we found ourselves surrounded, and I was taken prisoner. Cambyses wanted me to rule as his puppet, obedient to his commands. But I plotted secretly to resist the invasion: I was exposed, and for it I paid the price of my life."

"Tell me about the resolve of the Greek and Egyptian soldiers in the fight," demanded Thutmose III.

"No doubt, that of the Egyptians was immeasurably greater than the others," said Psamtek III.

"I expected to hear just that," Thutmose III affirmed. "Perhaps if your whole army had been Egyptian, the encounter would have turned out differently. But you disregarded your own people and relied entirely on foreigners—and so the history of independent Egypt ended at your hands."

"We cannot overlook that he refused to occupy the throne in the shadow of alien rule," Seqenenra intervened, "sacrificing himself by doing so. I myself shared such a fate."

"Before you stands my son, so blighted by misfortune," Isis implored. "He fought with all his bravery. If his ambition had been to rule at any cost, then it would have yielded to him. Instead, he died nobly and dearly."

Osiris bid him, "Go take your seat among the Immortals."

40

OSIRIS ADDRESSED the court:

"Members of the tribunal, now we are done with Egypt of the pharaohs. This court is not concerned with passing judgment on foreign rulers, but considers them all accursed outsiders. Rather, it differentiates by degree between the good ruler and the corrupt. Accordingly, it shall render account for the Egyptians, whether their nationality was gained by heredity or earned through residence and loyalty of the heart. Our verdicts shall not be final in the case of Egyptians who accept a new creed, such as Christianity or Islam. Instead, our judgment shall be a sort of historical appraisal that we hope will be duly considered when the citizen is tried by his proper religious court in the Abode of the Everlasting.

"Now I leave it to Thoth, the Divine Recorder, to speak."

"Egypt of the gods and pyramids, of temples and enlightened consciences, came to an end," Thoth began. "Persian kings sat on the Golden Throne. They adopted our customs and worshiped our gods, but nonetheless the Egyptians despised them. The people rose up in rebellion, to be defeated and enslaved. Then Alexander came and invaded our country as a liberator, after which one of his commanders inherited Egypt—his dynasty established a state and a civilization. The foreigners took charge of all important activity, while the Egyptians lived in darkness, cultivating the land, content with their place in the world.

"That is, with the exception of the priests, who were left in control of religious affairs. Resistance movements exploded in the form of mass emigrations and riots, which were put down with great bloodshed and brutality. The Greek family's era ended with the reign of Cleopatra, and the nation went under a new foreign rule, that of Rome, which considered her but a province to be annexed for her grains. The country's situation worsened. Each time the Egyptians rose up against oppression, their revolt was crushed and their blood flowed freely. In the epoch of the Roman ruler Nero, Christianity entered Egypt, and a part of the population changed their religion. This religion did not spring from Egypt herself, as happened in the age of Akhenaten, but was imported from abroad. Those who embraced the new faith clung to a strict asceticism, many of them dwelling in desert caves in flight from despotic rule and the corruption of the world.

"The Roman government fought the new faith, raining spears down upon its converts until the reign of the Emperor Diocletian became known as the Era of the Martyrs. In the time of Theodosius, the emperor decreed that Christians would be under his protection. Thus the ancient religion knew its own martyrs too—though the majority adopted Christianity, forming a distinct sect within it. The spirit of religious zeal blended with patriotic fervor, together fomenting an uprising in demand of independence. In riposte, they met with torture and killing on a limitless scale.

"The conflict turned into a sectarian battle between the Egyptian Church and that of Byzantium, and the death-struggle continued, accompanied by the most intense forms of repression."

※

A weighty silence fell as Thoth read to the court. When he had finished, Osiris motioned to Horus, who called out, "Al-Muqawqas, governor of Egypt!"

A short, thickset man came in, covered in his shroud, walking forward until he stood before the throne.

Thoth then read aloud, "Governor of Egypt before and after the Byzantine Conquest. The Copts considered him an Egyptian. During his time, the Arabs invaded Egypt, and he reached an agreement with them to be rid of Byzantine control. Thus Egypt entered a new era, under Arab rule."

Osiris invited him to speak, so al-Muqawqas began, "I held power in Egypt before the emperor did. Despite my Greek origins, the Jacobite sect of Egypt was satisfied with me, and the Copts thought of me as being one of them. I made an accord with the Arabs, throwing out the Byzantines—and the terms were most favorable."

"How could have you consented to a foreign invasion?" asked Abnum.

"I say to you, they were benevolent invaders," al-Muqawqas replied. "Their leader, Amr ibn al-As, divided Egypt into districts, and put a Coptic governor at the head of each. The people felt relieved in a way they had not been for hundreds of years. He lifted the restrictions on religious practice, and the Copts worshiped their Lord in the manner in which they believed."

"Then they did not take it upon themselves to resist the intruders?" gasped Ramesses II.

"A minority cherished their country above all," answered al-Muqawqas. "Yet the principal goal of the Arabs was to proselytize a new religion, and to use the invasion to spread Islam."

"And did Egypt experience a new age of martyrdom?" queried Abnum.

"The Arabs preached their faith without compulsion," al-Muqawqas told him. "Those who held to their old one paid the head tax to do so."

"What is the actual difference between this religion and ours of old?" Khufu wondered.

"They believe in the Divinity's uniqueness," said al-Muqawqas.

"That is my God, as well as my religion—I always knew I would triumph in the end," boasted Akhenaten. "Tell me, how did the people accept this faith? In my lifetime only a handful believed in it, and they carried no weight."

"Let's not quarrel over the gods," implored Abnum. "Talk to me about how the peasants and laborers benefited instead."

"Amr ibn al-As annulled a great many arbitrary taxes, and conditions lifted for the poor."

"This man's policies restored our children's welfare in a way that cannot be denied," spouted Isis.

"We grant you a certificate of commendation," said Osiris, "that may be of benefit in your proper religious trial."

41

Horus hailed, "Pope Benjamin!"

A thin man of medium height came in, pacing forward until he stood before the throne.

Thoth, Scribe of the Gods, then recited, "They persecuted him with banishment in the desert. Amr ibn al-As released him when declaring freedom of worship and the eviction of the Byzantines."

Osiris bid him speak.

"Belief is what ennobles man—what gives him his dignity, his strength, and his path to God," said Pope Benjamin. "I endured what I did of Byzantine oppression without being shaken in my faith. Then I shut myself in a monastery in protest against humanity's descent into the abyss of tyranny and corruption. Then God willed that Egypt should find herself ruled by the sons of Ishmael—and that they should institutionalize the freedom of religion. Hence I once again exercised the Alexandrian papacy and the spiritual governance of the Copts."

"So the best thing that an Egyptian could wish for," reeled Thutmose III, "was a just foreign occupation!"

"Our people had spent roughly a thousand years huddled in their villages," said Patriarch Benjamin, "prostrate under alien dynasties, who ruled over them by force and the sword."

"Did you not use your spiritual authority to awaken the populace?" asked Abnum.

"I lived at the time of a new invasion," the patriarch explained, "one that brought religious liberty and which lightened the torments of the peasantry. The occupiers did not impose their religion upon us, so it would not have been appropriate to spread the spirit of rebellion."

"There is no blame for this man," advised Isis, "who lived in an age whose advantage belonged to others."

"There is nothing that our court can hold against you," determined Osiris.

42

HORUS HERALDED, "Athanasius the Egyptian!"

A waif-like man of medium stature walked in, wrapped in his winding sheet, until he stood before the throne.

Osiris then proclaimed, "This court is assembled to try Egyptian rulers. This man was not a ruler, yet he represents the return of Egyptians to government. Therefore, his testimony is not lacking in historical significance."

"I began as a translator of Coptic into Arabic," stated Athanasius, "when Coptic was the language of the treasury accounts. Egypt lived in peace and stability until the reign of the Caliph Uthman, whose policies divided the Muslims. They plunged into internecine strife, ending in his murder. The Muslims in Egypt were also divided, splitting into two groups— those who were loyal to Uthman, and the others, his opponents. Wars broke out between them, which the Egyptians suffered as they raged in the country, until the caliphate fell to Muawiya— who appointed our governors from among his followers. In general, we did not have the luck to have a ruler as gentle as Amr ibn al-As again.

"During the governorship of Abd al-Aziz Marwan," continued Athanasius, "there were some reforms, but he also obliged the priests to pay a one-dinar tax. After they were absolved of this duty, he levied a tax of three thousand dinars upon the patriarchate, instead."

"How did the priests and the patriarch react to that?" asked the Sage Ptahhotep.

"Their reaction was a Christian one, based upon love and peace, sublime over the demands of this world."

"They didn't plot a revolution, as their ancestors had against me?" wondered Akhenaten.

"The conditions overall were good," answered Athanasius, "if you compare them with what they were under the Byzantines. Yet we were angry when some members of our community converted to the new religion. To us, it seemed that they had blasphemed themselves for profit, in order to avoid paying the head tax on non-Muslims. They, in turn, alleged that Islam was nothing more than a Christian sect, and their embracing it was not an act of apostasy."

"You eased the way for them to change their original religion," Khufu rebuked Akhenaten, "and laid the foundation for the practice of trading in beliefs."

"There is nothing wrong with a person changing their religion," retorted Akhenaten, "if his principal reason for doing so is honorable and enlightened. Yet I am amazed that the Arabs were guided to my faith, when my own people had spurned it for generation after generation."

"I see no reason to defend this man," offered Isis, "so long as no one is accusing him of any offense."

"We wish you the best possible outcome, Athanasius," Osiris told him, "in your Christian tribunal."

43

Horus called out, "The Master Antanash!"

A square-built man came in, stalking in his shroud until he stood before the throne.

Osiris invited Antanash to speak.

"I took up the profession of scribe in Coptic due to my deep knowledge of the language," Antanash responded. "In the vice-regency of Abdullah, brother of Caliph al-Walid ibn Abd al-Malik, it was decreed that Arabic would replace Coptic in all official documents. I was fired from my job, which was taken by a man from Homs in Syria. Our governor, I knew, took bribes—though his religion forbade it. After him came Qurrah ibn Sharik, a total despot who sometimes burst into churches to stop the prayers."

"What happened to the pact of Amr ibn al-As?" asked Abnum.

"How quickly rulers forget their religion," answered Antanash.

"What did the people do?" followed up Abnum.

"We were not able to mount any resistance," admitted Antanash.

"I'm sorry that the pharaohs were no longer in power," said Ramesses II.

"I'm sorry for the people in the period that you have erased from history!" barked Abnum at Ramesses II. "As for the pharaohs, the majority of them were crueler to the people than foreigners have been!"

"I will not permit . . .," Ramesses II began to reply.

"I am the one who permits or does not permit," Osiris interrupted him.

For a moment, all were silent. Then Osiris turned to Antanash, "May you go with good fortune to your Christian proceeding."

44

Horus called out, "Damyana al-Suwayfiya!"

A woman of medium height came in, walking forward until she stood before the throne.

Osiris asked her to speak.

"A peasant from Beni Suef," Damyana told them, "I became a widow with one young son. At that time, the chief tax collector was Usama ibn Yazid, infamous for his cruel and arbitrary behavior. Usama ordered that every priest wear an iron signet ring on his finger, with his name engraved upon it, that he would receive from the tax collector to prove he had paid his due. He threatened to amputate the hand of anyone who disobeyed this rule. He also imposed a fee of ten dinars upon anyone traveling by boat on the river. My financial circumstances compelled me to voyage by sailboat, and it happened that my son—who was carrying my ticket—bent down to drink, and a crocodile snatched him. They would not let me go, despite the word of eyewitnesses, and I was forced to sell all that I had with me."

"The religion was Islamic, and the law was Roman," opined Ptahhotep.

"During the age of darkness, the peasant knew only gloom, whatever the oppressor's name, or his nationality," fumed Abnum.

"As the people's patience dwindled, they grouped as revolutionaries," Damyana resumed. "The uprising lasted until the caliph in Damascus died. Then things quieted down, in hope of a new policy."

"May the gods bless you for the first pleasing piece of news they've heard," lauded Abnum.

Osiris turned to her, "Let justice be your portion in your final trial."

45

Horus heralded, "al-Hajj Ahmad al-Minyawi!"

A tall, strong man walked in until he stood before the throne. Osiris bid him speak.

"Originally from the family of Mikhail al-Minyawi," Ahmad said, "God guided me to Islam, so I converted. I learned the Arabic tongue, and memorized the Noble Qur'an. Then I became a teacher, and the Lord enabled me to go on pilgrimage. In my day, Umar ibn Abd al-Aziz was caliph, one of the Right-Guided Ones among the earliest leaders of Islam. When the Copts complained about their treatment under Usama ibn Yazid, the caliph ordered his arrest and removal. Sent in shackles to the caliph, he died on the way. Usama's place was taken by Ayyub ibn Sharhabil, who was very pious, and who compensated the Copts for what they had suffered in persecution."

"Why did you switch to Islam?" asked Akhenaten.

"Belief erupts in the heart without any warning," said al-Minyawi.

"I believe you," said Akhenaten, "and no one can believe you like an expert such as me. But didn't my hymns have any-thing to do with your faith?"

"Your name was unknown till a thousand years after this man's time," Osiris informed Akhenaten.

"Maybe you just wanted to escape the head tax?" Khufu prodded him.

"No—there was a military commander, Hayyan ibn Shurayh, who demanded that even those who become Muslims pay the head tax. When this reached the caliph, he ordered it to be cancelled, and that Hayyan be given twenty lashes, telling him that God sent Muhammad as a guide, not as a tax collector."

"May success go with you to your Muslim trial," said Osiris.

46

Horus hailed, "Samaan al-Gargawi!"

A muscular man walked in, then stood before the throne.

Osiris invited him to speak.

"A blacksmith, descended from blacksmiths," said Samaan al-Gargawi. "At the start of the caliphate of Hisham ibn Abd al-Malik, the Copts rose up in revolt, in which I took part, losing my life in one of its skirmishes. Hanzala ibn Safwan was the governor then, a thoroughly oppressive character. He wasn't satisfied with just taxing the people—he taxed the animals as well! For this reason, he was removed when a rebellion broke out."

"I praise you as liberator and a son of the people," said Abnum. "But I do wonder what caused your uprising to fail?"

"The caliph's power was overwhelming," answered Samaan al-Gargawi. "We were a small, isolated people who had lost the martial spirit. And we lacked the participation of our brothers who had switched to Islam—which made them loyal to the caliph."

"This invasion from within had never happened before," replied Abnum.

"Go to your Christian trial," Osiris said, "with our praise and blessings."

47

Horus heralded, "Halim al-Aswani!"

A tall, withered man walked in his winding sheet until he stood before the throne.

Osiris requested his testimony.

"I was a fruits-and-vegetables seller from a large family, half of which converted to Islam. As it happened, the leadership of the Muslims had shifted to a new family—during my time there was a caliph called Abu Jaafar al-Mansur. A series of governors came in succession, none of them lasting more than a year, sometimes less. There was no chance for anyone to think of reform. Things deteriorated to the point that the Copts revolted in Sakha. Conditions got so bad that plague and famine reigned until the people were eating both their animals and each other."

"How did the Muslims fare in this?" the Sage Ptahhotep inquired.

"They suffered as we did," answered al-Aswani. "They grew so extremely bitter that they accused the governor of violating the sharia, the sacred law. Regardless of our religious differences, our feelings were united, but those in power were stronger than all of us together."

"If you had all adopted the faith of the One God, then that would have saved you," claimed Akhenaten.

"The problem was one of bread, not of God," Abnum corrected him.

"Perhaps you will find justice in your final trial," Osiris consoled him.

48

HORUS CALLED OUT, "Sulayman Tadros!"

A thickset man of medium height came in, walking until he stood before the throne.

Osiris asked him to speak.

"A skilled engraver," said Sulayman Tadros, "I lived through the rule of four caliphs: al-Mahdi, al-Hadi, al-Rashid, and al-Ma'mun. And tens of governors all in a row, most of them conquered by wantonness, bribery, and oppressiveness. In their day, numerous uprisings broke out, and in some of them the Copts—the native Egyptians—both Christian and Muslim, and the Arabs, would all unite against the persecution, cooperating with each other to drive it out. Finally, al-Ma'mun himself came to restore order, and justice prevailed. Conditions improved for all the people, whatever their religion."

"Did you join any revolutions?" asked Abnum.

"No, but I lost a son in one of them," Sulayman Tadros replied.

"Seemingly, things were moving in a new track," said the Sage Ptahhotop.

"You truly deserve our empathy," said Osiris. "Go to your final trial in peace."

49

HORUS HERALDED, "Musa, secretary to Ahmad ibn Tulun!"

A tallish man came in and stood before the throne.

Osiris invited him to speak.

"A Christian Copt," commenced Musa, "The Lord granted me knowledge and skill, and the viceroy, Ahmad ibn Tulun, chose me as his private secretary. He was not an Arab, but was appointed in the caliphate of al-Muatamid ibn al-Mutawakkil. Thereafter he sought to solidify his own rule of the country. It was not only as though Egypt had regained her independence, but had annexed Syria and parts of Asia Minor, as well. He resolutely strove for reform and development, while upholding piety and justice, spreading his protective umbrella over the Muslims, Christians, and Jews alike—they all extolled his praise. He would sit for two days each week with those who had been wronged, just as in the days of the Right-Guided Caliphs.

"That is why, when Ibn Tulun fell very ill, everyone came out to the top of the Muqattam Mountain. The Muslims brought their Qur'an, the Christians their Gospels, and the Jews their Torah, all praying for his recovery!"

"Did the Coptic Christians profit by working for the governor?" asked the Sage Ptahhotep.

"His choosing me proved that he believed in religious equality," answered Musa. "So sure was I that he did believe in it, that even when I proposed Christian engineers to build his mosques and fortresses, I was looking for the right people, not playing favorites. The just ruler will extract the best from his helpers, and be an example to them."

"And how were the relations between the sects?" asked the wise Imhotep, vizier to King Djoser.

"Very good indeed, as is only appropriate in the reign of a fair-minded ruler," said "During Ibn Tulun's rule, Egypt became one single people, but of three religions. And Islam began to spread more, and to gain more converts."

Thoth, Scribe of the Gods, sought permission to pose a question—and it was granted. "Why did Ibn Tulun imprison Patriarch Michael of Alexandria?" he asked Musa.

"That was not his fault," Musa replied, "but a plot by a malicious archbishop named Sakka, who told Ibn Tulun that the patriarch was hoarding enormous wealth, far beyond his needs. So Ibn Tulun demanded that Michael give up part of his treasure at a time when the viceroy was girding to fight off foreign armies. When the patriarch said that he did not have such sums to give, he was arrested on a charge of treason. But then Ibn Tulun's son, Khumarawayh, succeeded him: he discovered the truth and set Michael free, and brought him back to his post with honors.

"But the heirs of Ibn Tulun were neither as strong nor as iron-willed as him. Fortune turned against their state, and Egypt again looked to the future with anxious eyes."

"You have presented a splendid account," Osiris told him. "May peace go with you."

50

HORUS HAILED, "Ali Sundus!"

A powerfully built man of middling height walked in, halting before the throne.

Osiris asked him to speak.

"A water carrier, I lived most of my life under the Ikhshidid rulers," Ali Sundus told the court. "Egypt had gone back to the fold of the Abbasids—and again, scores of viceroys came and went in succession, each inflicting injustices upon the Egyptians, whether Christians or Muslims. Finally, Muhammad al-Utfayh, a Mamluk descended from the kings of Farghana, took up our affairs. He made Egypt independent, and called himself 'the Ikhshid,' the customary title among the kings in his country. He drove away those who had designs on Egypt, and in each of his campaigns, urged the Christians to fight alongside him.

"Then power passed to his vizier, the eunuch Kafur, who called himself 'al-Ikhshidi' too. During his reign, Egypt possessed both the Hijaz and Syria. He purged the land of corrupt officials, and the nation flourished under his rule."

"How could you tolerate being ruled by a castrated slave?" said Ramesses II.

"All that mattered to us as Muslims," replied Ali Sundus, "is that he was a fair servant. A just slave is better than an oppressive prince."

"And just how does a slave surpass a prince?" Ramesses II answered rhetorically.

"By worshiping the One God," lectured Akhenaten. "All my life I appealed for human equality—only to be told that I was mad."

"May peace be with you in your Islamic proceeding," said Osiris to Ali Sundus.

51

HORUS CALLED OUT, "Ibn Qulaqis!"

A short, flabby man walked in and stood before the throne. Osiris bid him address the court.

"I am Abul Fatah Nasrallah ibn Abdullah, known as Ibn Qulaqis al-Lakhmi al-Iskandari, nicknamed 'the Mighty Judge.'"

"A name longer than those of most pharaohs!" gasped Osiris.

"My job was to moor the tall-masted ships at harbor, but I was also a poet. I visited the Maghreb and Sicily, praising their rulers in verse, just as I praised the Fatimids and the kings of Yemen. Egypt was my country, Islam was my homeland, and the art of praise my boon fortune. Hence my ode in panegyric to Yasir ibn Bilal, which opens thus:

> Sail ever onward to your great fate / The infant crescent has grown to full moon
> The water is kind to him who skims it / But evil to him who settles.

"And it is I who also said:

> Gaze on the sun as over the Nile it's sinking—
> More amazing when followed by the redness of evening."

"Tell me about the time in which you lived," Osiris ordered him. "Poetry is judged in another venue."

"The Ikhshidid dynasty was overturned by the Fatimids without resort to war," Ibn Qulaqis obliged Osiris. "They founded Cairo and al-Azhar, and improved the administration—bringing prosperity along with their reign. When al-Muizz li-Din Illah arrived, he received the nation's elite, among them Ahmad ibn Tabataba, the scientist and man of letters. He asked the new caliph, 'From whom did his lordship descend?'

"Al-Muizz then drew his sword half-way from its scabbard. 'This is my lineage,' the caliph replied, distributing gold to those assembled. 'And this is my nobility,' he told them. To this they answered, 'We have all heard and will obey.'"

"Why didn't you make your country independent after the Ikhshidids disappeared?" asked Abnum.

"And why didn't we split away when there was more than one Muslim caliph?" Ibn al-Qulaqis asked in return. "Independence means nothing to the Muslim—all he wants is a strong Muslim ruler who is also just. This we found under the Fatimids."

"When they swore their allegiance through gold and the sword?"

"Can there be a state without those two things?" Ibn Qulaqis again asked. "The Fatimid age was crammed with knowledge, art, and construction, while the Christians enjoyed both trust and security. But the rule of al-Hakim bi-Amr Illah was unforgettable for its clashing contradictions. Once he would favor the Muslims and persecute the Copts, another time he would coddle the Copts while bashing the Muslims, and then he would just be horrible to them all. But their era ended in a deadly famine—their awe and glory were wiped away, as the people were struck with stunning calamities."

"Proceed to your trial with peace," Osiris said to Ibn Qulaqis.

52

Horus heralded, "The vizier Qaraqush!"

A squat man walked in and stood before the throne.

Osiris invited him to speak.

"With the decline of the Fatimids," Qaraqush replied, "Salah al-Din al-Ayyubi came to Egypt to create a new state and the Ayyubid dynasty. Working as his vizier, I witnessed his reforms inside the country—in bettering the administration, reducing the poll taxes, and enforcing justice. Likewise I saw his accomplishments abroad—in uniting the Arabs and waging war successfully against the foreign Christians. His uprightness among the knights made him a model of bravery, chivalry, honor, and greatness, while in all my own labors I strove to improve government and make it more fair. Yet I was called a despot, without the least basis in fact, for forcing the removal of many dwellings while building the wall around the city of Cairo. No just person has ever known such injustice as I have."

After seeking permission to speak, Thoth asked him, "Did you not strip stones from some of the pyramids to build your great wall, without respect for what the ancients had done?"

"I removed some worthless pagan ruins," Qaraqush retorted, "in order to build for the sake of God and His prophet."

"The grandchildren have forgotten their grandparents' religion," lamented Khufu. "They're concerned with the present, not with the past."

"I consider them as believing in my God," Akhenaten answered Khufu.

"Salah al-Din's successors were not his equals," Qaraqush continued. "Christians from the north came to seize their glory. Damietta fell to them; they killed the men of Rosetta and desecrated the women. But in the end, they were defeated and left the country."

"The Ayyubid dynasty departed too," added Isis, "the good and the bad along with it."

"Take our thanks to your final trial," Osiris said to the vizier Qaraqush.

53

Horus hailed, "al-Shihab al-Khafagi!"

A squat, excessively fat man came in, padding ponderously until he stood before the throne.

Osiris asked him to tell his story.

"I was born in Syracuse," said al-Shihab al-Khafagi, "and grew into a man of language and letters. Among my most famous stanzas:

> For how long will his avoidance make war on me?
> My patience has only increased his soldiery.
> My ecstasy makes mock of me
> Just as his promises toy with my fantasies.

"I lived during the age of the Mamluks," he continued, "whom the Ayyubids acquired because of their beauty. They gave them a brilliant upbringing to be their own servants, passing on their property to them. Some of them became mighty sultans as well as excellent Muslims, prizing justice and order combined. But the majority was profligate and greedy, and the people suffered agony, poverty, and ignominy at their hands."

"I never realized that mamluks—slaves—had an age named after them," said Thutmose III.

"You recited some love verses for us," said the Sage Ptahhotep. "Didn't the torments of the people move your passion for poetry, as well?"

"In a letter, I wrote," replied al-Shihab al-Khafagi,

The good and virtuous have all gone—none remains
but those who take pride in rottenness and corruption,
in the spirit of pessimism, and the fruit of rebuke—
the successor to the owl, the sign of bad fortune.
Forbearance and silence are prolonged. How Heaven
wept for the earth when she lost a dear one, and the
clouds sobbed along with her.

"For hundreds of years the people lived through torments
and rapacity, and if not for Islam, they would all have perished
and disappeared."

"What did you say about the Mamluks?" wondered Abnum.

"I tried not to stretch my neck under their swords," answered
al-Shihab al-Khafagi.

"What was the role of Islam, which you have talked about?"
asked the Sage Ptahhotep.

"It was the brave ones among the men of religion," said al-
Shihab al-Khafagi, "who at times stood up to the tyrants in defense
of the wretched, and their efforts were crowned with success. The
downtrodden found in their faith both hope and consolation."

Osiris looked at the Immortals in their seats.

"Ladies and gentlemen," he addressed them, "I feel your
sadness and your rage as well. Therefore I want you to know
that our proceeding shall call out through the void to appeal to
the two courts—Christian and Muslim—to bring the harshest
possible penalties down upon all the iniquitous rulers who have
usurped the throne of the pharaohs."

Then he fixed his gaze on al-Shihab al-Khafagi.

"Go in peace to your final trial," he told him, "with neither
commendation nor censure from ours."

54

THOTH, SCRIBE OF THE GODS, read aloud, "When the Mamluk state vanished, Egypt fell as booty into the hands of the Ottomans. Hundreds of pashas came and went as governors over the country, the Ottoman army and the remnants of the Mamluks sharing control with them. Under them, Egypt knew ease and comfort but rarely, and for fleeting periods only. A deadly struggle broke out within the ruling regime, and assassination and treachery became the norm. The people drowned in worry, ignorance, and humiliation, a condition that lasted some hundreds of years."

Horus then called out, "Ali Bey al-Kabir!"

A muscular man of imposing height came in, walking in his winding sheet until he stood before the throne.

"You are the first foreign ruler that we have summoned to our trial due to the clearly Egyptian tendency in your policies—a kind not seen before. Hence I invite you to address the court."

"I started as one of the mamluks belonging to Ibrahim Kakhiya," said Ali Bey al-Kabir. "He prized me for my courage—so I became one of the few who were given the title of 'bey.' Next I became 'sheikh al-balad,' or head of the provincial government. At this point I thought of making Egypt independent of Ottoman rule, and I did just that. Immediately the hardships upon the people lessened. I was a just ruler, reigning righteously in accordance with Islam, and the Egyptians were blessed with peace and security—Muslims, Christians, and Jews as well. My domain stretched over the whole of the Arabian Peninsula, the Levant, and Nubia. If not for the treachery of Muhammad Abu al-Dhahab, one of my closest mamluks, Egypt's fate would have been different. Yet I died nobly, just as I had lived."

"Was not your making Egypt independent a violation of the unity of Islam," complained Akhenaten, "the religion of the One God?"

"The Ottomans were tyrannical and corrupt, under a phony Islamic façade," replied Ali Bey al-Kabir. "I was horrified by the torment that the Egyptians lived through. There was nothing for me to do but to make them happy under the shield of true Islam, if only by getting the Ottoman boot off their necks."

"I want to begin by thanking you for retrieving part of my empire," said Thutmose III.

Amenemhat I then said impatiently, "Didn't you benefit from my *Teaching*, which I imparted after a conspiracy hatched by some of those who were the very closest to me—and which nearly devoured me as its victim?"

"Actually, I had never heard of it. Whatever I needed was found in the Qur'an and the Traditions of the Prophet—though precaution cannot thwart fate."

Osiris then welcomed him, "For all that you deserve a seat among the Immortals—we shall note this in our certificate on your behalf."

55

Horus heralded, "Al-Sayyid Umar Makram!"

A straight-backed man, neither tall nor short, entered the court in his shroud, walking onward until he stood before the throne.

Osiris invited him to speak.

"I was born in Asyut," recited Umar Makram, "and learned science, morals, and religion from the flower of the elite. Then I became chief of the association of the Prophet's descendants, indefatigably repelling the powerful in defense of the suffering people. When the French came to invade our country, I called on the people to fight, and marched at their head, but our armies were routed and the French occupied Cairo. They chose me as a member of their local council, but I refused with contempt and escaped to Syria, leaving my money and property exposed to theft. When the French overran Syria, Napoleon brought me back to Egypt, heaping honors upon me, but I shut myself in my house. Then Cairo rose up in revolt, and I led the rebellion myself. After it was put down with brutality, I again left for Syria, and did not return until the French had gone.

"Next I directed the insurrection against the Mamluks, and another against the Turkish governor. I swore allegiance to the latter's replacement when I saw that he inclined toward the Egyptians, as well as toward justice and probity. But I resisted even that governor when he forgot his compact with us—and he forced me to leave once more. I remained in exile until I died."

"You are an individual from the people," Abnum addressed him, "who based his life on the defense of the people, calling on them to fight for the first time since my blessed revolution. They rose up against the foreign governor, and through their own power, installed a new ruler in his place. Tell me, was the new governor a son of the people, too?"

"No," Umar Makram replied, "but he was a Muslim, and he seemed just to me."

"What a catastrophe," recoiled Abnum. "Why didn't you try to take over yourself?"

"The Ottoman government would not agree."

"I tell you again, what a catastrophe," argued Abnum.

"Perhaps you simply revered the unity of Islam, the religion of the God Who is One?" suggested Akhenaten.

"Indeed," affirmed Umar Makram, "that is what I thought— as a believer in God and his Prophet."

"In any case, I am happy with this son," said Isis.

"You merit a place among the Immortals: your commendation from us shall state this clearly," assured him Osiris.

56

HORUS CALLED OUT, "Muhammad Ali Pasha!"

A stout, straight-backed, and powerfully built man strode firmly into the room until he stood before the throne.

Osiris asked him to speak, and Muhammad Ali recalled for the court, "I was born in the city of Cavalla, where I was raised as an orphan. Upon reaching manhood, I enlisted in the Ottoman army, and went to Egypt to join the fight against the French. When the French retreated, I began to study the conditions there and to ponder the future. Discovering the weakness of the Ottomans, and the meanness of the Mamluks, I became aware of a third force neglected by everyone, that being the power of the local people and their native leaders. I resolved to forge close ties with them, for perhaps they could form a sound base upon which to set up a new state that would bring back the glories of ages past.

"In this I scored an outstanding success, as the people ousted the Turkish governor and swore allegiance to me instead. The Sublime Porte recognized this *fait accompli* and all went well—so I set to work carrying out my project, not stopping once till the end of my life. I put paid to the prevailing evil of the Mamluks, then obtained an order from the imperial palace to wage war against the Wahhabis in the Arabian Peninsula—and vanquished them as well. I created an army made up of Egyptians, and conquered the Sudan. When my son Ismail was killed there, I avenged him by slaughtering twenty thousand of the enemy. For the army I set up academies and factories, just as I fashioned a formidable navy, employing the help of French experts to accomplish it all. Nor did I neglect reform, for I introduced new agricultural crops, such as cotton, indigo, and opium; I planted orchards and established parks. I also built medical schools and hospitals, and sent Egyptians on study missions to France, the land of modern civilization. I reorganized public administration and security, and among my most important monuments are the Khayriya Barrages. I also set up the first printing press in the Middle East, located in Bulaq.

"The sultan in Istanbul demanded that I campaign on his behalf in the Morea and Syria—and my victories were so stunning that terror beat in the heart of the Seraglio itself. The emperor wanted to keep me in my place, but I waged war against him, invading his country. I would have seized control of his capital were it not for the intervention of the foreign powers, who feared the revival of Islam at my hands. The nations conspired against me, forcing me to submit to the Sublime Porte's authority in return for making Egypt a hereditary fiefdom for my family. I was compelled also to reduce the size of my army and to close its schools and factories too. As the nation fell into ruin, I could not endure to the end: I lost my mind, then my life as well."

"This was like a new Pharaonic dynasty," remarked King Khufu, "despite its foreign origins."

"You restored my empire," said Thutmose III, "and I testify to your skill at military command. But you lost it in your own lifetime, making it the shortest-lived empire in history. Moreover, I'm amazed at your killing twenty thousand in revenge for your son's death, as though you had not heard of my own wise policy in the countries I invaded."

"I had never heard of it," Muhammad Ali admitted. "And in truth, no one paid any attention to the ruins of your age before the savants who accompanied the French invasion arrived in Egypt, unlocking the secrets of their forgotten tongue. I acquired my own wisdom through my direct dealings with people."

"I acknowledge your greatness," Thutmose III continued, "but by its light I see your delusions. I very much wanted to indulge you to the last, but for the regrettably rapid end that befell your empire. This means that, despite your intelligence, your perception of things was wanting. You did not grasp the international situation well enough, and thus unwittingly exposed yourself to a force that you could not control."

"I thought that France would stand by me until the end . . .," Muhammad Ali started to say.

"This, too, does not aid in your defense," Ptahhotep interrupted him. "A very short-sighted policy."

"Yet it was a tempting opportunity to renew Islam—the Islamic State rising from a rejuvenated Egypt."

"I comprehend that completely," enthused Akhenaten, "and I hail your ambition to reinvigorate the state of the One and Only Divinity."

"If only you had put your genius and your dreams to the strengthening of Egypt," lamented Khufu, "and contented yourself with that."

"You did not believe enough in the people," Abnum berated him. "Nor was your love for them sufficient for you to devote your real efforts to their revitalization and support. You exploited the peasants for the sake of the land and the state, when you should have set every institution at the service of the people. Yet only someone like me would think this way. However, one cannot forget in your favour that you also drove the peasants into the fields of administration, politics, the military, and science."

"For that reason," insisted Isis, "I consider this alien viceroy as one of my sons."

113

"If this were the court that would seal your final fate," Osiris addressed him, "it would hand you a harsh critique and a wounding rebuke—while preserving your right to a seat among the Immortals. Accordingly, we shall send a report to your Islamic trial in praise of your majestic achievements, conveying therein a recommendation on behalf of your person from Egypt and her gods."

57

HORUS HAILED, "Ahmad Urabi!"

A tall, corpulent man of dignified mien came in and stood before the throne.

Osiris invited him to speak.

"I memorized the Qur'an as a child in my village in al-Sharqiya," Ahmad Urabi replied, "and enrolled in the military academy at the age of fourteen. I attained the rank of Qaimqam, the first Egyptian to reach that level. The higher grades were reserved for those of Circassian origins—the Egyptians were scorned in their own country. I persuaded some of my colleagues to demand the dismissal of the minister of war, a prejudiced Circassian—and when we were arrested, the patriotic troops rose up to demand our release. I felt the people's sense of debasement, and moved with the army to Abdin Palace to insist on the king's abdication and the creation of a popular assembly.

"The khedive told me, 'I inherited this country as my personal fief, and who are you but slaves of our beneficence?' In reply I told him, 'God created us all free, not as possessions or real estate. By the God but for whom there is no other god, we will not be passed on as inheritance nor be enslaved after this day.'

"We were victorious over the enemies of the people, and established a popular assembly and a nationalist government, when the foreign powers intervened to prevent the people from controlling their own affairs, out of fear for their interests. The khedive and some of his opportunistic followers betrayed the homeland, coming to an agreement with our English foes.

Although we defended our nation with everything we had, we still were defeated. They sentenced us to exile for life, and the expropriation of our possessions."

"But you challenged the occupant of the throne," said Khufu, "and reproached him in ways that one does not do to kings!"

"Times change, O king, for monarchs no longer rule as the deputies of God," Osiris told him, "but with the participation of the people."

"Sharing power with the peasants means chaos," rebutted Khufu.

"Rather, it's a bold undertaking on the road to virtue," asserted Abnum.

"The khedive and his followers were foreigners," said Ahmad Urabi.

"The unity of Egypt was forged out of differing kinds of people," said Menes, "who all joined together to create a nation, and who were loyal to the throne."

"I only battled those who disdained from joining with the rest of us," explained Ahmad Urabi, "and the proof is that my party also had members of Circassian descent."

"Why didn't you kill the khedive," demanded Abnum, "and install a new royal family of commoner blood?"

"My goal was to liberate the people," answered Urabi, "and for them to share the responsibility of rule."

"It would have been better to kill him," repeated Abnum. "But, in any case, you get much credit for guarding the people's rights."

"The situation required military leadership of exceptional genius," said Thutmose II. "Unfortunately, you were not endowed with anything of the kind."

"I gave everything I had," pleaded Urabi.

"You should have fought until death alongside your troops," scolded Ramesses II.

"And you should have eliminated all your enemies in order to throttle treason in its cradle," added Abnum.

"You are a good-hearted man," said Akhenaten, "whose end was the one fated for all with this virtue."

"You launched a revolution to free the people—and gained a foreign occupation for them, instead," concluded the Sage Ptahhotep.

"This is a son of Egypt, whose heart is full of good intentions," said Isis. "He gave the people his limitless love and his limited ability. His foes plotted to put down his revolution—yet they could not extirpate the seed of freedom that he had planted in our good soil."

"I consider you a light beaming in the darkness that had descended on your country," Osiris told him. "You were punished during your lifetime and so have paid for your mistakes. Perhaps you will gain blessings in your final trial—we shall not withhold praise for the merit you have earned."

58

Horus called out, "Mustafa Kamil!"

A slender, sweet-featured man came in, with head uncovered and feet unshod, and stood before the throne.

Osiris invited him to speak.

"I came to consciousness as a pupil during the British occupation. I hated it and resolved to combat it—this is what I felt when only a student. One day, His Honor the Khedive, Abbas Hilmi II, came to visit our school, and I greeted him with a passionately patriotic speech that found an echo in his own youth and nationalism. From that time onward we became close collaborators, and he provided me with encouragement and money to be rid of foreign control. I developed similar relations with the caliph and the Islamic League. As for my own aspiration, it was always for the freedom and independence of Egypt—which is why I changed my relations with Abbas Hilmi when he reached a *modus vivendi* with the enemy.

"Things were such that the people had given up hope, but I did not stint from awakening their national awareness, through word of mouth, the press, and public speaking. Likewise I advocated the nationalist cause abroad, until the liberals of Europe—especially in France—knew of it as well. And when the British carried out their great crime in Denshaway, I denounced their vicious deeds and decried the sentences that the puppet court had pronounced on the innocent people of that village. I shook the throne of the English despotism in Egypt until I forced their nation to reconsider it. Then I founded the Nationalist Party, the first political party formed in Egypt. Its program called for the withdrawal of foreign troops and a constitution within the dominion of the Ottoman State. I kept on waging this jihad both inside and outside the country, until I gave up the ghost while still quite young."

"Didn't the British kill you?" asked Psamtek III.

"No, they did not," Mustafa Kamil replied.

"That is odd," said Psamtek III. "In my time we had the Persian occupation, just as you had the English in yours. Like you, I strove to arouse patriotic awareness—and when Cambyses learned of this, he ordered my execution without hesitation. How could the British let you go unpunished?"

"The occupiers had taken total control of the country," answered Mustafa Kamil. "They could afford to permit a certain degree of freedom that in fact they despised, but which made them look as though they respected such principles in the eyes of the world."

"But weren't you exposed to palpable harm?"

"The occupation concealed its hatred of me, while inciting its friends to attack me."

"Your age granted you clemency such as I did not receive even a part of in my own day," remarked Psamtek III. "In truth, I have never known a holy warrior as fortunate as you. You enjoyed the support of the khedive, the caliph, and the Islamic League, smiting your foes both at home and abroad without any penalty. You won glory and fame without paying a price, and were not slaughtered as I myself was. Nor were you exiled, like Ahmad Urabi."

"Ahmad Urabi was a traitor," spat Mustafa Kamil, "who drew foreign occupiers into the country."

"How can you accuse the man of treason when he did not rise in rebellion or endure banishment from his homeland except to defend the right of your people! And what was the traitor but the father of your friend, aide, and loyal supporter? Yet in your testimony he had betrayed his country, like his father before him."

"I consider him to be the foremost of those to responsible for the occupation," sneered Mustafa Kamil.

"You are an ardently patriotic lad," proclaimed Abnum, "you were lucky enough to live your life in the fragrant atmosphere of the throne, the caliphate, and French civilization, without smelling the odor of sweaty labor, nor suffering the pains of true struggle. Nor do you refrain from defaming a true revolutionary."

"He is a son that awoke nationalist zeal and enthusiasm," said Isis, "when the occupation had nearly snuffed them out."

Osiris then faced him.

"It was not in your power to do more than you did, and we shall not forget the favor in your words," he assured Mustafa Kamil. "Go to your final trial with our heartfelt regards."

59

HORUS HERALDED, "Muhammad Farid!"

A medium-built man with a plump face walked in, wearing nothing on his head or his feet, until he stood before the throne.

"Coming from an ancient, aristocratic family, I shared Mustafa Kamil's nationalist stance from the start. For this reason, I resigned from the government to devote myself to the patriotic cause above all else. My bond with Mustafa Kamil grew so strong that he named me as his successor to lead our party. I followed his ideology, his way of speaking to crowds and of writing, until I was arrested and tossed into prison. There they tried to persuade me to soften my position in exchange for a pardon, but I rejected any deal. After I got out, I was even more stubborn and refractory than before.

"I traveled throughout the country, making the case for nationalism, and they conspired to send me to prison with the leaders of the party. I decided to emigrate in order to carry on agitating from abroad. We crafted our escape at the right time and successfully got away. And as much as we were able to accomplish some things outside the country, the party was also subject to weakness and fragmentation within. We bore the bitterness of longing for Egypt and our families, and many people spurned us. Then the 1919 Revolution broke out back home, a totally unexpected revolt, one that never had occurred to my mind. It happened while I was forgotten in exile, while others sat on the leader's chair instead of me.

"We proclaimed our satisfaction with the movement's bosses without believing that most of them were sincere, congratulating the masses for their courage. We cheered the memory of their martyrs and urged them to hold steadfast until the end. My life ended while I was yet banned from returning to Egypt."

"A satisfactory leadership indeed, given what it faced in suppression," said Psamtek III.

"You could well have savored a voluptuous life," said the Sage Ptahhotep, "and high rank common to men of your wealthy class. But you left all that entirely and chose struggle and agony for the sake of Egypt. You are a great man indeed . . ."

"Tell me how a leader abandons his country in a time of disaster, to fight for it in a foreign land?" demanded Abnum.

"They planned to put us in prison," said Muhammad Farid.

"But the leader of the just cause knows that he is made for imprisonment or death," insisted Abnum, "not for waging his jihad abroad."

"Jihad outside the homeland had been a part of our nationalist strategy since the days of Mustafa Kamil."

"That was accepted as an auxiliary element to help complete the original mission inside the country," Abnum corrected him. "But for you and the rest of the leadership to leave your party with no actual leaders in your absence was anything but brave or wise behavior. The fact is, you were notables that I would have put to death in my own revolution without any mercy. You loved being patriotic leaders as well as the respect and position that this had brought you. Yet you couldn't deal with real struggle— and the detention, torture, or death that comes along with it. Instead, you ditched your duty when things got rough, in order to conduct a nice, safe holy war abroad. Doing so, you became responsible for the weakness and division that afflicted the nationalist movement.

"And so I was staggered by your surprise that a revolution had flared up among the people, though at the same time amazed at your lofty feelings of victimhood when they chose a leader other than you. You seem to have viewed the leadership as an inherited birthright that passes within your class like money and land—even after you've fled the field of battle."

"You're repeating what our enemies used to say!" exclaimed Muhammad Farid.

"I do not deny your patriotism," admitted Abnum. "But your love of Egypt was entwined with your deep-set contempt for the Egyptians. The feeling of loyalty to a nominal identity never left you, while inevitably your life turned to tragedy, because the leader of the people had to be of the people—one marked by human greatness, not aristocratic grandeur."

"As for me," spoke up Isis, "I see him as one of the best of my sons, in character, sincerity, and national feeling. Nothing more could be asked of him, considering the circumstances of his birth and upbringing."

"From us, you have a certificate backed by esteem and affection," Osiris promised Muhammad Farid. "Go to your final trial with our sincerest good wishes for a fortuitous verdict."

60

Horus hailed, "Saad Zaghloul!"

A towering, strongly favored, strikingly compelling, and awe-inspiring man entered the room. He kept on walking until he stood before the throne.

Osiris invited him to speak.

"I was born in Ibyana," he began, "and studied at al-Azhar as a pupil of Jamal al-Din al-Afghani. I worked as an editor at *al-Waqai al-misriya*, under the direction and tutelage of Muhammad Abduh. I joined the Urabists during their uprising, and at the start of the British occupation, I was jailed for belonging to the Vengeance Association. Leaving my job, I practiced law then became a judge. Later I was chosen as education minister, and after that, minister of justice.

"At the end of the First World War, with the declaration of the Armistice, I became the leader of the nationalist movement. I carried this out on the strength of the indivisible patriotic unity between Muslims and Christians, proclaiming Egypt's right to liberty and independence. The British authorities arrested me, and exiled me to the island of Malta. No sooner was this news broadcast than the people revolted in protest at my deportation, demanding an end to foreign rule. As a result, England was forced to set me free.

"I then traveled with the Wafd's delegation to Paris to present our case to the peace conference there, but its doors were shut in our faces. We entered into negotiations with Britain, but nothing came of them. Then the Wafd split internally, and I returned to

Egypt. Afterward I was exiled a second time, this time to the Seychelles Islands in the Indian Ocean. They did not release me until 1923.

"Following that, I served as prime minister after winning the popular elections in 1924. I went right into negotiations with Britain again, which promptly failed. Then, after the assassination of one of the English commanders, I was forced to step down.

"The political parties arrayed themselves in harmony against the king's dictatorship, and I became speaker of the People's Assembly, leaving the premiership to the Liberal Constitutionalists. Talks with the British began once again—but I departed the world before knowing their outcome."

"I undertook the first popular revolution," boasted Abnum, "at the end of the Old Kingdom, and, after thousands of years, you started the second one. You are my brother and my dear friend."

"There is a difference between the two revolutions that we must keep in mind," cautioned Khufu. "Abnum's revolt was by the common folk against the cream of society, while Saad Zaghloul's revolution pitted all of Egypt's people, rich and poor alike, against the alien occupation."

"I think that wealthy people are not fond of revolution," opined Abnum.

"From the first, I was eager to preserve our unity," said Saad Zaghloul, "for strength is indispensable when facing the enemy. Yet I became convinced that the rich hated the revolution more than the occupation."

"You should have got rid of them," Abnum upbraided him.

"They broke away from me," answered Saad Zaghloul, "plotting their own path to independence that matched their point of view."

"But you united the Egyptians, just as I unified their kingdom," said Menes to Zaghloul. "For that reason, you are my comrade and my successor, as well."

"Regardless of the leadership you showed after the revolution," commented Imhotep, vizier to King Djoser, "you consented to work in government before the revolution, in the shadow of the occupation, without joining the National Party. How do you explain this?"

"The National Party advocated fantastical ideals," Saad replied. "One could not negotiate until after the withdrawal of foreign forces from the country. That would mean that the occupation would last forever. Another was to refuse to take public office while the British dominated these positions. Yet in my opinion, it wasn't enough to demand a particular kind of behavior from people. What you demand must be practical for general application, without prejudice or indifference to their needs. Mustafa Kamil was able to boycott government appointment because the khedive was providing him and others with money, while Muhammad Farid could do the same due to his vast private holdings. But what could the party's followers do? If they obeyed their leaders, they would go bankrupt, and if they deviated, they would be forced to betray their pact. How could one preach a lofty principle that people would find so difficult to live up to, that would instill such feelings of guilt in them? And how could you leave the public postings to foreigners?

"I accepted official life as an instrument of resistance in service to the nation, which needed it most urgently. My adversaries admitted this before my friends did."

Here Osiris interrupted, admonishing all assembled, "For those who would like to read it, this leader's deeds are written in the record. But here in this court, we will discuss only actions of a fateful nature."

Then he interrogated Saad Zaghloul directly, "Your enemies claim that the revolution took place while you were in exile, and that you did nothing to instigate it yourself. Rather, you were astonished that it happened, as though it had taken you by surprise. What do you say to that?"

"The country was in a state of despair," answered Zaghloul. "I admit that I was caught off guard when the revolution began, just as the man who had been leader before me, Muhammad Farid, was too. Yet I did not refrain from preparing the atmosphere for it with speeches on all possible occasions, and in meeting with people in my house, in the countryside and in the cities, urging them to support my position, filling them with patriotic feeling. Moreover, the revolution erupted in reaction to my exile, and so my person provided the spark that ignited it."

"Such a critical position usually demands a particular type of behavior," declared Abnum. "The effective leader is the one who is able to serve as the model for such action. The situation here demanded sacrifice, for that is the most that an unarmed people can put up against an overwhelming power. When Saad confronted the enemy and they forced him into exile, he set the desired example, and the people followed it by launching the revolution. What testifies to Saad's greatness is that he accepted this sacrifice while despairing of any revolution to protect or defend him—and his sacrifice was total. Noble bravery, when there was no hope for any kind for survival. If he had had hope for the revolution, then his grandeur would be lesser in the degree of his enormous self-denial."

"Some also say," Osiris continued, "that the bias in your leadership drove the intellectuals from being supporters of you into breaking away from you. How do you answer that?"

"In truth, I lived only for the revolution: I believed in it completely. Through it I discovered my cherished goal, which I had sought for all my life. As for the intellectuals, they hated and feared the revolution, contenting themselves with spurious solutions. They had money, experience, and sophistication, but their patriotism was impure, just as their faith in the people was lacking."

"Some of your followers felt that you should have remained as head of the revolution," Osiris reminded him, "rather than accepting the post of prime minister."

"My premiership was an extension of the revolution at the cabinet level," Zaghloul asserted.

"I think it would have been better if you had considered the view of these supporters," Abnum insisted.

"May the gods bless this great and righteous son," beamed Isis, "who has proved that Egypt's people possess a strength that cannot be vanquished, nor ever die."

"You are the first Egyptian to rule the country since the age of the pharaohs," said Osiris, "and you did so by the will of the people. For this reason, I grant you the right to sit among the Immortals, who are your forebears, until the end of this trial. Then may you go in peace to your proper proceeding, bearing our commendation, and our sincerest good wishes."

And so Saad Zaghloul took his place among the Imperishable Ones in the Hall of Sacred Justice.

61

Horus heralded, "Mustafa al-Nahhas!"

A firmly framed man who was not quite tall walked onward until he stood before the throne.

Osiris asked him to address the court.

"I was born to a poor family in the Delta town of Samanud," said Mustafa al-Nahhas. "With intensive effort, I completed my education. Due to my outstanding performance, I was appointed a judge and learned justice and righteousness. I joined the Nationalist Party, with whose president I had been a student colleague in the Khedivial College. And when the Wafd formed under the leadership of Saad Zaghloul, he chose me as a member—and I was banished with him to the Seychelles in 1921. I took part in his populist revolutionary cabinet, and when he died, I was elected chief of the Wafd.

"I bore the burden of the struggle on the path to independence and a democratic life for a quarter of a century. I was prime minister seven times, resigning six times due to differences with the English and the king. In 1936, under the pressure of the threat of a world war, I accepted a coalition with the other parties, reaching a pact with the British, who recognized the independence of Egypt and promised the withdrawal of their troops in 1956.

"The Second World War broke out during a period of arbitrary royal rule in Egypt. The king was accused of making contact with the enemies of the English, and a grave political crisis erupted, as the British contemplated removing the monarch. I put myself forward to save the nation and the throne, and

129

created a ministry under the most arduous conditions. And when the war ended and the English were victorious, I planned to demand their immediate withdrawal—but the king discharged me. He returned to his absolutism, and things went from bad to worse, until he was compelled to agree to a popular referendum, and I came back as prime minister in 1950.

"I then negotiated with the British over their withdrawal, but meeting no response, I abrogated the treaty of 1936 and declared that they must depart. My enemies inside and outside the country plotted against me, and the king was able to be done with me. With the 1952 Revolution, I was forced to quit politics, until eventually I passed away."

"Those present would like to know some of your accomplishments while you served as prime minister," said Osiris.

"Though the people were not in power for more than eight years, in contrast with eighteen years of autocratic rule by the king and the minority parties," replied Mustafa al-Nahhas, "and despite what they suffered in repression, and the repeated attempts to assassinate me, God permitted me to render not a few services to our country. Among these were the repeal of the foreign capitulations, the abolition of the Religion Fund, the establishment of the Arab League, the independence of the judiciary and the national university, the civil service law, the ban on foreigners owning agricultural land, the first compensation for on-the-job injuries and mandatory insurance against them, the recognition of labor unions, the requirement that foreign companies use the Arabic language, the social insurance program, the creation of the general accounting office, and free primary, secondary, and intermediary education."

"Welcome to the third revolutionary leader in the history of our people," lauded Abnum. "He extended his power through his faith in his people and his God. His life was poisoned by prolonged struggle and strife. He lived a poor man, and died one as well."

"Please accept my love, O leader," said Akhenaten. "You are like me, who was completely identified with the belief in the One God, and devotion to the pure principles. You are like me also in your love of the people's humbleness, and in your mixing with them without any sign of arrogance or condescension. And like me, you were subjected to the enmity of the scoundrels and the worshipers of power, and the prisoners of self-interest, both living and dead. And you are like me in that you were fortunate to experience of the ecstasy of victory, and also tested by way of rejection and defeat. But be glad—for in the end, the victory is ours!"

"This is a decent man," declared Isis, "one of our most righteous sons."

"I grant you the right to sit among the Immortals until the end of this proceeding," decided Osiris. "Then you may go to your final trial, bearing with you our most generous commendation."

62

HORUS CALLED OUT, "Gamal Abdel Nasser!"

A tall man entered; his features were strong and his personality powerful. He continued to stride forward until he stood before the throne.

Osiris asked him to state his case.

"I come from the village of Beni Murr, in the districts around Asyut," Abdel Nasser said proudly. "I was raised in a poor family, from the popular classes, and endured the bitterness and hardships of life. I graduated from the War College in 1938, and took part in Wafdist demonstrations. I was besieged along with the others at Falluja in 1949. The loss of Palestine dismayed me, but what disturbed me even more was the depth of the defeat's roots inside the homeland.

"Then it dawned on me that I should transfer the fight to within, where the real enemies of the nation were hiding in ambush. Cautiously and in secret, I formed the Free Officers' organization. I watched as events unfolded, waiting for the right moment to swoop down upon the regime in power. I realized my objective in 1952, then the Revolution's achievements—such as the abolition of the monarchical system, the completion of the total withdrawal of British troops from the country, the breaking up of the big landed estates through the law of agricultural reform, the Egyptianization of the economy, and the planning for the comprehensive revamping of both farming and industry to benefit the people and to dissolve the divisions between the classes—came one after another. We erected the High Dam while creating the public sector on the path to building social-ism. We built a powerful, modern army. We spread the call for Arab unity. We assisted every Arab and African revolution. We nationalized the Suez Canal. In all this we were a beacon and a model for the entire Third World in its struggle against foreign colonialism and domestic exploitation. In my time of rule, working people enjoyed strength and power not known to them before. For the first time, the way was made for them to enter the legislative assemblies and the universities as well, when they could feel that the land was their land and the country their country.

"But the imperialist forces lay waiting to spring upon me—and then the detestable defeat of June 5, 1967 descended upon me. The great work was shaken to its foundations, and I was doomed to what seemed like death three years before I actually expired. I lived a sincere Egyptian Arab, and died an Egyptian Arab martyr," Abdel Nasser ended his opening statement.

"Allow me to convey to you my vast love and admiration," gushed Ramesses II. "What is my affection for you but an extension of my love for myself? For look how much we resemble each other. Both of us radiate a greatness that filled up our own country till it spilt over her borders. Both of us fashioned a surpassing victory from a defeat, while neither of us was satisfied with his own glorious accomplishments, raiding the deeds of our predecessors as well. To my good fortune, I sat on the throne of Egypt when she was supreme among nations, while you ruled when she was a tiny band of believers straggling amongst titans. The God bestowed strength of spirit and body upon me through all my long life, while begrudging you but a little of these things, hastening your demise before your time."

"Your interest in Arab unity was higher than your interest in Egypt's integrity," bemoaned Menes, "for you even removed her immortal name with one stroke of the pen. You compelled many of her sons to migrate abroad, such as happened only in fleeting moments of subjugation."

"I am not to blame if some Egyptians see Arab unity as a catastrophe for themselves," disputed Abdel-Nasser, "nor if I accomplish majestic things that those who came before me were too weak to achieve. For in truth, Egyptian history really began on July 23, 1952."

A hubbub arose among those present, continuing to build until Osiris called out, "Order in the court! Ladies and gentlemen, you must allow everyone to express their opinion freely."

"Permit me to hail you in my capacity as the first revolutionary among Egypt's poor," began Abnum. "I want to testify that the wretched did not enjoy such security in any age—after my own—as they did in yours. I can only fault you for one thing: for insisting that your revolution be stainless, when in fact the blood should have run in rivers!"

"What is that butcher raving about now?" objected Khufu, scowling.

"Do not forget that you are no longer sitting upon your throne," Osiris berated him. "Say you are sorry."

"I am sorry," said Khufu sheepishly.

"Despite your martial upbringing," Thutmose III lectured Abdel-Nasser, "and though you have proven your outstanding ability in many other fields, none of them were military. Nor were you a military leader in any serious sense of the term."

"One must forgive my defeat by an army equipped by the most powerful state on the face of the earth!"

"Your duty was to avoid war and to refrain from provoking superior powers!" Imhotep, vizier to King Djoser, rebuked him.

"That conflicted with my goals, while I was deceived more than once!" Abdel-Nasser complained.

"An excuse worse than the offense," snapped Ptahhotep.

"You attempted to blot my name from existence, along with the name of Egypt," said Saad Zaghloul. "You said about me that

I rose on the crest of the 1919 Revolution. Let me tell you about the meaning of leadership. Leadership is a divine gift and a popular instinct. It does not come to a person either by blind luck or chance. The Egyptian leader is the one to whom all Egyptians pledge their allegiance, regardless of their differing faiths—or he will never be leader of the Egyptians. He may also be an Arab or Islamic leader—for which, in any case, I don't reject your claim. I consider your slander against me but a youthful indiscretion, that perhaps could be tolerated in view of the glorious services you have rendered. The Urabi Revolution was a noble struggle that was thwarted most painfully. The 1919 Revolution was one of the great exploits bestowed by history, but its enemies grew more and more numerous until it was wiped out with the burning of Cairo. Then your revolution came, and you put paid to its enemies as you completed the message of the two earlier uprisings. And though it began as a military coup, the people nonetheless blessed it and gave it their loyalty. It was in your power to build its base among them and to establish an enlightened, democratic form of government. But your delusive impulses toward autocracy were responsible for all the drawbacks and disasters of your rule."

"We needed a period of transition to fix the foundations of our revolution," Abdel-Nasser asserted.

"That is a feeble dictatorial claim that we always hear from the nation's enemies," Mustafa al-Nahhas, Zaghloul's successor as head of the Wafd Party, retorted scornfully. "You had at your disposal a popular Wafdist fundament which you crushed with your tanks. You were incapable of creating an alternative to it, and the country suffered in a vacuum instead. You stretched out your hand to the criminals of the land, falling into an unfortunate contradiction between a reforming project whose spirit had come from the Wafd, and a style of rule inspired by the king and the privileged elites—until this way of running things frustrated all your fairest designs."

"True democracy to me," swore Abdel-Nasser, "meant the liberation of the Egyptians from colonialism, exploitation, and poverty."

"You were heedless of liberty and human rights," al-Nahhas resumed his attack. "While I don't deny that you kept faith with the poor, you were a curse upon political writers and intellectuals, who are the vanguard of the nation's children. You cracked down on them with arrest and imprisonment, with hanging and killing, until you had degraded their dignity and humiliated their humanity, until you had had eradicated their optimism and smashed the formation of their personalities—and only God knows when their proper formation shall return. Those who launched the 1919 Revolution were people of initiative and innovation in the various fields of politics, economics and culture. How your high-handedness spoiled your most pristine depths! See how education was vitiated, how the public sector grew depraved! How your defiance of the world's powers led you to horrendous losses and shameful defeats! You never sought the benefit of another person's opinion, nor learned from the lessons of Muhammad Ali's experience. And what was the result? Clamor and cacophony, and an empty mythology—all heaped on a pile of rubble."

"I moved my country from one condition to another, just as I shifted the Arabs and the course of helpless nations. The problems will be treated until they disappear. In time, they will be forgotten, while what was helpful to humanity will remain. Then the people will affirm my true grandeur."

"If only you had been more modest in your ambitions, if only you had stuck to reforming your nation and had opened the windows of progress to her in all areas of civilization. The development of the Egyptian village was more important than the world's revolutions. Encouraging scientific research was more urgent than the campaign in Yemen. Combating illiteracy was more imperative than confronting global imperialism. Unfortunately, you wasted an opportunity that had never appeared to the country before. For the first time, a native son ruled the land, without contention from king or colonizer. Yet rather than curing the disease-ridden citizen, he drove him into a competition for the world championship when he was hobbled by illness. The outcome was that the citizen lost the race, and himself, as well."

Here Isis had her say.

"My joy at the return of the throne to one of my children cannot be contained!" she exclaimed. "His magnificent accomplishments would need all the walls of the temples in order to record them. As for his faults, I do not know how to defend them."

Osiris then announced his verdict.

"If our trial here had the last word in your judgment," he declared, "we would be compelled to give long and difficult consideration to arrive at justice. Certainly, few have performed so many services to their country as you have for yours, nor brought down so many evils upon it as you have, as well. However, in your case, being the first of Egypt's sons to occupy her throne since olden times, and the first to devote himself to the laboring people's welfare, we will suffer you to sit with the Immortals until this tribunal ends. Afterward, you shall go to your final trial with an appropriate recommendation."

63

Horus heralded, "Muhammad Anwar Sadat!"

A trim, dark-complected man of middling stature came in. He continued on his way until he stood before the throne.

Osiris invited him to address the court.

"I was born in the village of Mit Abul-Kom," Sadat began, "and raised in a poor family. There I met with many daunting hardships during my studies. Filled with patriotic passion since I was small, I took part in Wafdist demonstrations. I was able to enroll in the War College, which opened its doors to people of lowly backgrounds like mine after the treaty of 1936. From the time of my graduation, I was appalled that the army was under the control of the British military. Seized by the idea of armed revolution against the English, I created the first secret apparatus in the army in 1939. I contacted the Muslim Brotherhood and was much impressed by their activities; during the war, I also tried to be in touch with the Germans. For that I was arrested and put on trial. Not only was I acquitted, I was returned to military service, as well.

"At that time, Gamal Abdel-Nasser contacted me and recruited me to his organization. When the 1952 Revolution occurred, events kept cascading one after another until Abdel-Nasser died, and I succeeded him as president in a moment of acute crisis. I was well aware of the negatives that decayed the greatness of the Nasser era, so I launched a new revolution to save the nation from imminent doom. I smashed the centers of power, then moved slowly toward establishing security and democratic rule. On October 6,

1973, I surprised not only the occupying enemy, but the whole world with an unforeseen victory. I achieved a triumph that saved the Arab soul from despair as it redeemed honor from shame, before embarking on another adventure by boldly entering the enemy's land to call for a settlement between us using words rather than weapons. My long quest ended with the accords at Camp David. I launched the great opening, al-Infitah, to rescue the nation's economy, and made new advances toward representative government. Yet I was hindered by obstacles that I had not taken into account, for the opposition deviated from the true path, as the fanatic religious tendency suddenly began to menace the nation with violence. In the face of all these challenges, I adopted a resolute position from which there could be no retreat—but matters ended in my assassination on the anniversary of the day on which I had brought my country the pride of victory."

Akhenaten was first to reply to Sadat's speech.

"I hail you as a fellow apostle of peace," he told him. "Nor am I astonished at your opponents' accusing you of treason. They made the same charge against me, and for the same reason."

"Your victory reminds me of that of Ramesses II, which culminated in a pact of peace and the marriage of his son to the daughter of the Hittite king," said Thutmose III.

"A ruler is responsible first and foremost for the life of his people," added Ramesses II. "From this starting point, he resorts to war or turns toward peace."

"I sincerely believed in the futility of continuing a war policy," said Anwar Sadat.

"How much you resemble me, Mr. President," Amenhotep III admitted, "in your love of the good life for your people and yourself. Both of us reveled in pageantry and ease, in grandeur and palaces. Yet my age allowed me to bask in luxury without vexation, while in yours you tasted the bitter with the sweet. Permit me to express to you my sympathy and my affection."

139

"You ruled in circumstances similar in some respects to those which confronted me during my first reign," Horemheb said, "after the death of the aged King Aya. I concede that you performed truly noble deeds, and that you took some beneficial steps. Yet you were so lax in combating corruption and corrupt people, that it seemed your victories were turned into defeats."

"I labored to encourage civil servants to strike off the hands of corrupt officials," swore Anwar Sadat.

"No nation can exist without discipline and morals," proclaimed Horemheb.

Then Gamal Abdel-Nasser asked Sadat, "How could it have been so easy for you to distort my memory so treacherously?"

"I was forced to take the position that I did, for the essence of my policy was to correct the mistakes I inherited from your rule," rebutted Sadat.

"Yet didn't I delegate power to you in order to satisfy you, encourage you, and treat you as a friend?"

"How tyrannical to judge a human being for a stand taken in a time of black terror, when fathers fear their sons and brothers fear each other!" shot back Sadat.

"And what was the victory that you won but the fruit of my long preparations for it!" bellowed Abdel-Nasser.

"A defeated man like you did not score such a triumph," retorted Sadat. "Rather, I returned to the people their freedom and their dignity, then led them to an undeniable victory."

"And you gave away everything for the sake of an ignominious peace," bristled Abdel-Nasser, "dealing Arab unity a fatal thrust, condemning Egypt to exclusion and isolation."

"From you I inherited a nation tottering on the abyss of annihilation," countered Sadat. "The Arabs would neither offer a friendly hand in aid, nor did they wish us to die, nor to be strong. Rather, they wanted us to remain on our knees at their mercy. And so I did not hesitate to take my decision."

"You exchanged a giant that had always stood by us for one who had always opposed us!" Abdel-Nasser upbraided him.

"I went to the giant who held the solution in his hand," pointed out Sadat. "Since then, events have confirmed that my thoughts were correct."

"Then you rushed into the Infitah until the country was drowning in a wave of inflation and corruption," Abdel-Nasser asserted, pressing his indictment. To the degree it was possible, in my time the poor were secure, while in yours, only the rich and the thieves were safe."

"I worked for the well-being of Egypt, while the opportunists pounced behind my back," lamented Sadat.

"You tried to murder me, and, if not for Divine Providence, you would have succeeded," said Mustafa al-Nahhas. "Yet you lost your own life as the result of assassination. Do you still believe in that method?"

"We need to live twice to acquire true wisdom," pleaded Sadat.

"I have heard of your call for democracy, and I was astonished," al-Nahhas continued. "Then it became clear to me that you wanted democratic rule in which the leader has dictatorial authority."

"I wanted a democracy that would return the village to its traditional manners, and bring back respect for the father," said Sadat.

"This is tribal democracy," al-Nahhas replied.

"That is true," said Saad Zaghloul. "Yet, though true democracy is taken, not given, there is no call to blame him unreasonably."

"The travails of the people grew worse and worse," resumed Mustafa al-Nahhas. "What happened is what usually transpires in such conditions, when one avoids dealing with strife and extremism. You let things get out of control as if you didn't care. Then suddenly you exploded and threw everyone in prison, enraging both Muslims and Christians, moderates and extremists alike. Finally things culminated in the tragedy at the reviewing stand."

"I found that there was no other option but a decisive blow to control the chaos," Sadat said defiantly, "for it seemed the country was about to erupt into full-blown civil war."

"When the ruler usurps the rights of his people, he makes an enemy out of them," adjudged Saad Zaghloul. "When that happens, the political strength of the country is squandered in internal conflict, rather than in doing what should be done."

Isis then uttered her summation.

"Thanks to this son," she said, "the spirit returned to the homeland. Egypt regained her complete independence, as it had been before the Persian incursion. He erred as others too have erred, while accomplishing more good than others have done."

Osiris then turned toward Anwar Sadat.

"I welcome you as one of the Immortals among the sons of Egypt," he told him. "You shall proceed to your other tribunal with a testimonial bestowing honor from ours."

64

Osiris directed his gaze toward the Immortals.

"Thus has the life of Egypt passed before you in all its joys and sorrows," he intoned, "from the time that Menes brought forth her unity, until she regained her independence at the hand of Sadat. Perhaps, then, some of you have reflections that you would wish to mention now?"

King Akhenaten sought leave to speak.

"I appeal to you to hold to the worship of the One God," he called out, "for the sake of truth, immortality, and liberation from the idolatry of earthly things."

"Be zealous for the unity of the land and the people," admonished Menes, "for disaster only comes when this unity is ruptured."

"Egypt must believe in labor," declared Khufu, "for with it I erected the Great Pyramid, and by it all things are built."

"And she must believe in science," implored Imhotep, the vizier of King Djoser, "for that is the force behind her immortality."

"And in wisdom and literature," seconded the Sage Ptahhotep, "to savor the vitality of life and to imbibe its nectar."

"And she must believe in the people and in revolution," preached Abnum, "to propel her destiny toward completion."

"And believe in might," said Thutmose III, "that cannot be achieved before she has grappled with her neighbors in battle."

"And that government be of the people and for the people," exhorted Saad Zaghloul.

"And that relations between people be based on absolute social justice," demanded Gamal Abdel-Nasser.

"And that her goal be civilization and peace, as well," added Anwar Sadat.

"May the Divinity be implored," Isis sighed hopefully, "to invest the folk of Egypt with the wisdom and the power to remain for all time a lighthouse of right guidance, and of beauty."

All opened their palms in supplication, absorbed in prayer.

Translator's Afterword

BEFORE THE THRONE IS NOT MERELY a book about olden times. This is a tableau of all Egypt's history, from the remotest past to practically the present, and the rulers who led her through it— each judged by the Osiris Court, which in the ancient religion decided the fate of the soul after death. Moreover, its author insisted that this work (published as *Amam al-'arsh* in 1983), was not fiction. When pressed on the matter, Naguib Mahfouz, whose own life (1911–2006) spanned nearly a century, replied simply, "It is history."[1]

But if so, it is history of a peculiar kind. Though based on many years of research and a lifetime of reflection on Egypt's past, the setting is imaginary and the dialog invented. And far from being conventional historical fiction, or even romance, like his first three published novels (all of which were set in ancient Egypt), this is actually a kind of theatrical conversation between characters, with scant stage directions and the barest of scenery, though we are told that the décor is all of solid gold.

Why did Mahfouz choose this particular allegorical device? And why did he want to render an historical verdict upon so many of Egypt's rulers? His exposure to classical literature, dating back to his studies of Greek thought published as a young man (obtaining a degree in philosophy from the Egyptian University, now Cairo University, in 1934), and his lifelong self-study of Egyptology may provide the answer.

Inspired by the explosion of Egyptian patriotism that sparked the 1919 movement for national independence led by

Mahfouz's lifelong hero, Saad Pasha Zaghlul 1859?–1927),
and by the global frenzy at the discovery of Tutankhamun's
tomb in 1922, Mahfouz's first published book was a translation
of a brief work on ancient Egypt aimed at young readers by
the British scholar, the Rev. James Baikie, in 1932. Though
Mahfouz wrote dozens of short stories set in contemporary
Egypt, a small number are set in, or use motifs from,
Pharaonic times (now collected in English translation in *Voices
from the Other World*). The action of his first three novels—
Khufu's Wisdom (*'Abath al-aqdar*, 1939), *Rhadopis of Nubia* (1943)
and *Thebes at War* (*Kifah Tiba*, 1944), likewise occurs in ancient
Egypt. Yet, each, in its own way, obliquely critiques contemporary Egyptian politics—especially the last of these, an allegorical attack on both the British and the Turkish aristocracy.[2]
But with his next two novels, *al-Qahira al-jadida* the latter published in English as *Cairo Modern* and *Khan al-Khalili*, both set in
the twentieth century and both possibly published in 1945, he
discovered that the risks of censorship were slight, and aban-
doned a plan to compose forty novels on ancient Egypt to
focus instead on life in his own times. Thus he ultimately
created such contemporary masterpieces as *The Cairo Trilogy*—
Palace Walk, *Palace of Desire*, and *Sugar Street*) as well as scores of
other works in a breathtaking array of styles and genres.[3] He
did not return to the Pharaohs for nearly forty years—with
Before the Throne.

Among his wide readings from ancient Egyptian literature as
a young man, Mahfouz later confessed that a Middle Kingdom
poem, *The Dialogue of a Man and His Soul*, had deeply impressed
him.[4] In it, an unnamed man contemplates death, debating its
merits and demerits with his *ba* (a spiritual element released
after death that connects the deceased in the burial chamber
with the celestial deities).[5] The man tells the story, recounting
his arguments in favor of earthly life against his *ba*, which

defends the advantages of death as though speaking in a court of law before an audience that may include the gods.[6]

Another possible source for the concept of presenting the afterlife trials of earthly movers and shakers is found in the writings of Lucian, a Hellenized Syrian in the Roman administration at Alexandria in the mid-to-late second century AD. Lucian cleverly adapted the judgment of the dead by the Greek underworld court headed by Zeus' son Minos in order to mock the world of the quick. In his *Dialogues of the Dead*, the infamously irreverent Diogenes of Sinope (d. approximately 325 BC) invites one of the Cynic philosophers to join him in the House of Hades, lord of the shades:

> "Diogenes bids you, Menippus, if you've laughed enough at the things on the earth above, come down here, if you want much more to laugh at; for on earth your laughter was fraught with uncertainty, and people often wondered whether anyone at all was quite sure about what follows death, but here you'll be able to laugh endlessly without any doubts, as I do now—and particularly when you see rich men, satraps and tyrants so humble and insignificant, with nothing to distinguish them but their groans, and see them to be weak and contemptible when they recall their life above."

As John Rodenbeck writes, the "satirical dialogues and fantastic tales" of the "long-lived Lucian of Samosata . . . have spawned many imitations." Dialog as a means to convey abstract argument was itself key to the ancient Greek philosophy that Mahfouz had read.

Both Plato and his mentor Socrates asserted, Anthony Gottlieb notes in his book *The Dream of Reason*, that "truth emerged only through dialogue," and Plato's works were all "at least ostensibly" in that form. This could also explain why Mahfouz's only published forays into writing for the theater—a series of short plays that he produced intermittently following the cataclysmic Arab defeat of 1967—were really just dialogs, with little or no stage directions or descriptions. Though he loved every aspect of drama, including the omnipresent singing and dancing of Egyptian productions (he apparently didn't miss an opening night in Cairo's theater district until at least the mid-1960s), Mahfouz the playwright nonetheless dispensed with everything but raw verbal confrontation between characters. He evidently felt that only ruthless dialog could unflinchingly expose the existential truths behind the naked humiliations and despair of the time.

A further potential model for *Before the Throne* is an allegory in prose on the fate of the soul by the blind Syrian poet Abu al-'Ala' al-Ma'arri (d. 1058). In al-Ma'arri's *Risalat al-ghufran* (The Epistle of Forgiveness), a shaykh enters the afterlife—but in imagination only—to see how the drunkard poets of the Pre-Islamic "Age of Ignorance" have managed to find divine forgiveness.[7]

Or he may have read a work similar to that of al-Ma'arri's, *Risalat al-tawabi' wa-l-zawabi'* (Treatise of Familiar Spirits and Demons), by an Andalusian late contemporary, ibn Shuhayd (d. 1035), who "meets the spirits of a number of prominent littérateurs—poets such as Imru' al-Qays, Abu Nuwas, Abu Tammam, and al-Mutanabbi, prose writers such as 'Abd al-Hamid, al-Jahiz and Badi' al-Zaman al-Hamadhani—and critics," in the other world, as described by Roger Allen.[8]

Perhaps a more immediate literary example of a trial involving Egypt's former rulers is Sir H. Rider Haggard's "Smith and the Pharaohs." In this story, an English archaeologist, accidentally locked in the Egyptian Museum overnight, finds himself witness to a ghostly assembly of the kings and queens whose bodies and belongings are housed in the building. After overhearing them gossip about the performance and relative merit of their respective predecessors and successors, he finds himself brought before them for formal judgment as a despoiler of the royal dead.

And yet another contemporaneous precedent—which Mahfouz may well have read—is George Sylvester Viereck's eccentric 1937 biography of Wilhelm II, *The Kaiser on Trial*, apparently ghost-written by "Essad Bey," a Jewish-cum-Muslim writer (later "Kurban Said," born Lev Nussimbaum in Baku). Essad Bey was a popular novelist and nonfiction author based in both Weimar and Nazi Germany who was also widely read in the rest of Europe, the U.S., Central Asia, and the Middle East. He died in Italy in service to the Axis in 1942. Tom Reiss, Essad Bey's own biographer, sketches the essential details of this oddly path-breaking book:

> *The Kaiser on Trial* is a bizarre historical pastiche written in the form of courtroom testimony. It is ostensibly the trial of the Kaiser for war crimes in front of a tribune of historical figures, both dead and living. It is also a reflection on the first years of the twentieth century and the events that ended the [sic] Europe's old empires in a vast spectacle of mass killing and destruction. George Bernard Shaw praised it as an effective "new method in the writing of history," providing "a mine of information . . . both dramatic and judicious."[10]

Mahfouz also had more occult sources of inspiration—and even wrote a kind of prototype of *Before the Throne* in the form of a long (49 pp.) short story, "The Seventh Heaven" ("*al-Sama' al-sabi'a"*) in 1979. In "The Seventh Heaven," a series of famous figures, ranging from Pharaoh Akhenaten (1353–1336 BC), Saad Zaghlul, Vladimir Ilyich Lenin (1870–1924), Gamal Abdel-Nasser (1918–1970), and others, face brief afterlife trials conducted by a former Egyptian high priest from ancient Thebes, in their quest to reach the highest (seventh) level of Paradise. Strikingly, in this work influenced by the writings of the Egyptian spiritualist, Ra'uf Sadiq Ubayd,[9] no one—not even Adolf Hitler or Joseph Stalin—suffers eternal damnation, only brief spells of penance back on earth. Hitler himself returns as a petty crime *capo* in a Cairene alley. (For this and other tales of the uncanny by Mahfouz, see his collection, *The Seventh Heaven: Stories of the Supernatural*, translated by Raymond Stock, AUC Press, 2005). Many of the Egyptian characters make their afterlife encores in *Before the Throne*.

And in *Before the Throne*, more striking than even the glittering visual splendor of the supernatural backdrop is Mahfouz's choice of the Osiris Court as the vehicle for delivering his own historical judgments. God of the afterlife and chief of the tribunal that judges the souls of the deceased, Osiris is one of ancient Egypt's oldest known deities, his roots sunken and decayed in the mud and clay of the northeastern Delta. An ancient folk belief held that he was an actual—and prodigious—king in Predynastic times (a view still debated by Egyptologists), but the first known image of him dates to the Fifth Dynasty, one of many minor deities grouped around the king, "with a curled beard and divine wig in the manner of traditional ancestral figures."[11] In the Old Kingdom, he was associated with the royal dead only, mainly in the great necropolis of Abydos in Upper Egypt, though gradually, his popularity grew. His nemesis was Seth, who eventually became an Egyptian prototype of Satan, the Evil One. In one of Pharaonic Egypt's most famous myths, Seth twice attacks Osiris, the second time cutting him up into sixteen pieces and throwing them into the Nile. All the pieces are recovered by his sister–wife, the goddess Isis, except one—his penis.[12] That critical lacuna aside, one should note that, to the ancient Egyptians, "the dying of Osiris does not seem to be a wrong thing," as Herman Te Velde says, "for death is 'the night of going forth to life.'"

Crucial to *Before the Throne* is the role Osiris plays in the passage of the dead into the next world—or into nonexistence. In the ancient myth,[13] Osiris, in the shape of a man wrapped in mummy bandages, bearing the symbols of royal power (the elaborately plumed *atef* crown on his head, a false beard on his chin, the crook and flail in his hands crossed over his chest), presided. Meanwhile the jackal-headed god of embalming, Anubis, introduced the deceased and weighed his or her heart on a great double-scale against a feather representing *Ma'at*, the principle of divine order and justice. If the defendant had committed no grave sins on earth, the heart would balance with the feather— and the deceased would be pronounced "true of voice" (a con- cept that resonates strongly in Mahfouz's work) and given the magic spells necessary to enter the underworld, *Duat*.

But if there was no balance with the feather, the heart was fed to "the devourer," Ammit, a terrifying female beast with the head of a crocodile, the body of a lion, and the hind legs of a hippo. As all of this transpired, the ibis-headed Thoth, god of writing and magic, supervised and recorded the judgments and reported them to Osiris. (Another representation of Thoth, a baboon, sat atop the scale.) Meanwhile Isis (a radi- antly beautiful woman with either a throne—which was her emblem—or a solar disk and horns upon her head),[14] her son, the falcon-headed Horus (who introduced and pleaded for each defendant), and other deities looked on.

The Osiris Court, carved and painted in tombs, and depicted on papyrus in the *Book of the Dead*, is the most vivid and enduring image from old Egyptian beliefs regarding the fate of the individual after death. It has even been found, crudely but beautifully displayed, on the gilded cartonnage covering the chests of Roman-era mummies excavated by Zahi Hawass at the Bahariya Oasis in 1999 (and later). The artisans who made them came from a society that had already forgotten most of the other elements of ancient Egyptian religion—including, apparently, even the knowledge of how to correctly write the sacred (hieroglyphic) script.

Perhaps further proof of the Osiris Court's persistently haunting imagery is that Mahfouz, who had set aside Pharaonic Egypt as a central setting or theme in his fiction for nearly forty years, then seized upon it as the framework for one of his strangest and most explicitly ideological books. In *Before the Throne*, subtitled *Dialogs with Egypt's Great from Menes to Anwar Sadat*, Mahfouz dramatically presents his views on many of Egypt's political bosses from the First Dynasty to the current military regime. And he does so by putting words in their mouths as they defend their own days in power before the tribunal of Osiris. *In Before the Throne*, those whom Mahfouz sees as the greatest leaders of ancient Egyptian civilization, under the aegis of the ancient Egyptian lord of the dead, judge those who followed them, from the unification of the Two Lands through late antiquity and the Middle Ages, right to his own times. This continuum of Egyptian history showcases his essentialist vision of a sort of eternal Egyptian *ka* (the living person's undying double who, in the afterlife, receives mortuary offerings for the deceased, thus ensuring their immortality).[15]

From pharaohs to pashas, and from prime ministers to presidents, only those who serve that great national *ka*—according to Mahfouz's own strict criteria are worthy of his praise—and a seat among the Immortals. The rest are sent to Purgatory (the counterintuitive destiny, in chapter 22, of the youthful king whose tomb's discovery spurred the young Naguib's love of ancient Egypt)—or even to Hell (like the hapless governor Nesubenedbed in chapter 32).

That he used an ancient Egyptian mode of judgment (albeit his own version of it) to hold these leaders to account, rather than a more conventional setting speaks loudly of his conviction that Egypt is different and must look to herself for wisdom—as well as offer it to the world. The Immortals even proclaim an Egyptian "ten commandments" in the final chapter.[16]

Despite the historical mission behind *Before the Throne*, some of the characters are seemingly the products of Mahfouz's mind—and his need to invent voices for a cherished idea. An outstanding example is Abnum, who emerges as the leader of the "rebels of the Age of Darkness" (the First Intermediate Period) in chapter 5, and thereafter throughout the book as the bloody-minded champion of the oppressed. Mahfouz claimed that Abnum, who embodies the right of the common people to rise up against injustice, was a real figure he'd found in his research.[17] Yet I have found no trace of him in the available sources that the author likely consulted, while the 'revolution' he allegedly led probably never occurred, at least not in the way that Mahfouz portrays it.

Mahfouz also uses terms, both religious and racial, that some readers might find strange. To him, historically, 'Copt' means 'native Egyptian' (derived from *Aegiptos*, the name the Greeks gave the country in antiquity), though today it refers to the indigenous Christian minority, who are thought to be the most direct descendants of the ancient Egyptians.

More confusingly, Mahfouz sometimes refers, not to God (in the monotheistic sense), or the gods (in the pantheistic one), but to a being called 'the God.' This partly reflects Mahfouz's knowledge of the ancient Egyptian practice of adopting local divinities as objects of special devotion, and the worship of certain gods such as Amun, Horus, Khnum, Osiris, Ptah, and Ra as deities linked to kingship. For example, Ramesses II (chapter 26) invokes Amun—without naming him—as a patron, protective god when cut off by the Hittites at Kadesh. Moreover, Mahfouz, like many of his fellow Muslims, tended to view the ancient Egyptians as proto-Muslims, who would have regarded each minor god as but a manifestation of a grand single godhead. (In chapter 21, Imhotep even enunciates the kernel of this idea to Akhenaten—whose role as the first known monotheist made him the subject of Mahfouz's 1985 novel, *Akhenaten: Dweller in Truth*).[18] Nonetheless, many characters speak of the various gods as actual beings. Above all, Mahfouz employs the conceit of the Osiris Court, with four of the ancient deities very much active in it (though shorn of their famous physical attributes), perhaps—but not necessarily—representing aspects of God. To finesse the theological conundrum this creates, the ancient gods do not render final judgment on defendants from the Christian and Islamic eras, but leave that task to a higher authority.

Just as curiously, the author's view of international relations seems to be based on ancient Egyptian logic. Though he praises his hero Saad Zaghlul as well as several Pharaohs, such as the doomed Seqenenra (chapter 10) and Psamtek III (chapter 39) and others for bravely fighting foreign occupation, Mahfouz paradoxically loves Egypt as an empire, lauding such conquerors as Amenhotep I (chapter 13), Thutmose III (chapter 17), and Muhammad Ali (chapter 56)—though the latter was not a native Egyptian. Whether aware of it or not, here Mahfouz demonstrates the divide between what the ancient Egyptians saw as *Ma'at* and its opposite, *Isfet* (chaos, hence injustice). In their conception, foreigners were always inferior to Egyptians (though an Egyptianized foreigner would be accepted among them). Thus Egypt's control and even seizure of neighboring lands in the Near East and Nubia were considered a fulfillment of *Ma'at*, while an alien power invading Egypt was the triumph of evil over the proper cosmic order.[20] Hence Mahfouz bars all but a few non-native rulers who either had become Egyptian or otherwise acted in Egypt's best interest from the right to trial and thus the chance for immortality in *Before the Throne*. Indeed, the work as a whole seems but an expression of Mahfouz's own personal version of *Ma'at* as embodied in his nation's history.

Whatever its original source, this paradoxical attitude toward empire and occupation is remarkably similar to that of the "Pharaonists," a group of intellectuals in the 1920s and 1930s to which Mahfouz belonged. Led by such luminaries as Ahmad Lutfi al-Sayyid (1872–1963), first rector of the Egyptian University, Taha Hussein (1889–1973), the great blind Egyptian *belles-lettrist* and novelist, and Mahfouz's "spiritual father," the Coptic thinker and publisher Salama Musa (1887–1958)—the Pharaonists believed that Egypt was both much older and much closer to Europe and the Mediterranean in culture than her Arab and African neighbors.[19]

While his fellow Egyptians largely rejected this idea by the 1940s, Mahfouz did not—at least not completely. Though in his 1988 Nobel lecture,[21] delivered for him in Stockholm by Mohamed Salmawy, he declared himself "the son of two civilizations" (the Pharaonic and the Islamic) to the Swedish Academy which awarded the prize, Mahfouz never quite roused himself to the same level of zeal for pan-Arabism or pan-Islam when they became the intellectual vogue in later years, despite enormous peer pressure, and numerous attempts of his own, to get there."

A sensitive and problematic issue is the treatment of Jews (who are mentioned only three times as a group: twice in chapter 49 and once in chapter 54, in the trial of Ali Bey al-Kabir—Ali Bey the Great), as well as Egypt's often rocky relations with both ancient and modern Israel. Mahfouz, who as an adolescent grew up in a largely Jewish area of suburban Abbasiya, once told me, "I really miss" the Jews of Egypt,[22] all but a few of whom were dispersed from the country in the 1950s and 1960s.

Though the king most often theorized to be the pharaoh of the Exodus—a story found in similar form in both the Old Testament and the Qur'an—is given his own trial in *Before the Throne* (Merneptah, chapter 27), the tale itself is neither told nor even mentioned. Israel by name appears only once (in the trial of Pharaoh Apries, chapter 37)—briefly (and fatally) aligned with Egypt against the Babylonians—while Judah is captured by Egypt in the trial of Pharaoh Nekau II (chapter 35).

In *Before the Throne*, the current State of Israel does not exist at all except as the formidable but unnamed enemy whose presence dominates much of the proceedings in the final two trials (62 and 63). These are of Gamal Abdel-Nasser, champion of the Arab masses who led them into the catastrophic defeat of 1967, and Anwar Sadat (1918–1981), the "Hero of War and Peace" whose initially successful surprise attack on Israeli-held Sinai in October 1973 revived Egypt's pride—and whose later bold gambit of peace with the Jewish State would finally cost him his life. Yet, with the successful pacts of peace signed between Seti I (chapter 25) and his son, Ramesses II, and the Hittites, Egypt's aggressive military rivals based to her northeast, one of the main aims of *Before the Throne* clearly is to justify the 1979 Camp David Peace Treaty that Sadat signed with Menachem Begin.[23]

In the end, the tribunal apparently feels that Sadat has won the debate. Osiris invites Sadat to sit with the Immortals— though he had only *permitted* Nasser to do so. The presiding deity had sent Nasser (who had infuriated the court by declaring that "Egyptian history really began on July 23, 1952," the day of his Free Officers coup) on to the final judgment with but what he termed 'an appropriate ("*munasiba*") recommendation.' Sadat's testimonial, however, was qualified as "*musharrifa*," or "conferring honor."

Mahfouz's defense of Arab–Israeli peace would cost him a great deal, including boycotts of his books and films for many years in the Arab world. And it may have contributed to the attempt on his life by Islamist militants on October 14, 1994, roughly the sixth anniversary of the announcement of his Nobel. Though it is believed the attack was in punishment for his allegedly blasphemous novel, *Children of the Alley* (*Awlad haratina*, 1959),[24] it fell on the day that Yasser Arafat, Shimon Peres, and Yitzhak Rabin were revealed to have won the Nobel peace prize in Oslo.[25] Then, and even now, accused by some of selling out to Israel (which has no demonstrable influence over the Swedish Academy) for the sake of his prize—despite devoting most of his Nobel lecture, cited above, to a defense of Palestinian rights, and even endorsing Palestinian suicide bombings—he nonetheless never renounced his support for Camp David and the dream of a true, lasting, and comprehensive peace between Arabs and Jews someday.[26]

Regardless of one's own views, by the breadth of its historical vision and the painstaking attempt to literally narrate Egypt's continuous cultural, political, and religious identity throughout the long life of the country, *Before the Throne* justifies Rasheed El-Enany's praise of Mahfouz as the "conscience of his nation." And, one could add, he sought to be her memory as well.

True to his mission, a few years later, Mahfouz sought to balance his books (literally and figuratively) by attacking Sadat's Open Door economic policy (*al-Infitah*) and its disastrous effects on Egypt's poor and middle classes in his brief novel, *The Day the Leader was Killed (Yawm qutila al-zaʿim)*.[27] Published in 1985—four years after Sadat's assassination by Islamist extremists—it was so harsh on the martyred president that Mahfouz paid a call on his widow, Jehan Sadat, to reassure her that he had not meant the work to rationalize his murder. Evidently without a sense of irony, he told her: "It's only a novel—not a work of history."

X

Though most of Mahfouz's works are about the world in which he lived, there remains, wrapped mummy-like within his massive oeuvre, both a deathless love for his nation's ancient past and a persistent quest for insight into the afterlife—a quest as old as Egypt herself (and no doubt much older). Though we have lost him among us, he has since fittingly gone to his own place in the west (which the ancient Egyptians saw as the land of the dead) in both Pharaonic and Islamic style—a handsome brick tomb, with a stela bearing Qur'anic verses in its ground-level chapel[28]—in a modern cemetery southwest of Cairo on the road to Fayyum. Meanwhile, his immensely rich and varied literary legacy reminds us of the wisdom in the New Kingdom tome, *Be a Scribe*:

> A man decays, his corpse is dust,
> All his kin have perished;
> But a book makes him remembered
> Through the mouth of its reciter.
> Better is a book than a well-built house,
> Than tomb-chapels in the west;
> Better than a solid mansion,
> Than a stela in the temple![29]

Mahfouz, clearly, was more than a scribe (in the modern sense, though Egyptologists use it to mean all literate people in the Pharaonic age), a mere recorder of ledger items and lists. In *Before the Throne*, he ceased to be a teller of imaginary stories, as in most of his fiction. Rather, he became a kind of historian—even a righteous judge of the dead—personally choosing who was worthy of a hearing, the evidence presented, and their sentences as well.

Here, the ultimate verdict was his. We can only hope that the Supreme Judge dealt with him as fairly, and according to the same principles—which placed the love and welfare of Egypt (as he saw it) over all others—in his own final trial.

Ж

The translator would like to acknowledge Roger Allen, Hazem Azmy, Peter Blauner, Brooke Comer, Humphrey Davies, Johannes den Heijer, Abdelasiem el-Difraoui, Mourad el-Shahed, Ismail El Shazly, Mona Francis, Gaballa Ali Gaballa, Nermeen Habeeb, Fredrik Hagen, Melinda K. Hartwig, Zahi Hawass, James K. Hoffmeier, Salima Ikram, W. Raymond Johnson, Shirley Johnston, Mary A. Kelly, Klaus-Peter Kuhlmann, Joseph F. Lowry, Yoram Meital, Bojana Mojsov, George Nazzal, Richard B. Parkinson, Adham Ragab, Donald Malcolm Reid, Bruce Redwine, Tawfik Saleh, Ahmed Seddik, David P. Silverman, Sasson Somekh, Rainer Stadelmann, Peter Theroux, Kent Weeks, David Wilmsen, and especially Husayn Ukasha, for their generous assistance, as well as Noha Mohammed, Nadia Naqib, Kelly Zaug, R. Neil Hewison, and Randi Danforth of the American University in Cairo Press for their always-excellent editing. Most of all, I wish to thank my mother, Helen Stock, who passed away in 2007, as well as the also-departed author—who made this wonderful project possible.

This translation is dedicated to Mariangela Lanfranchi.

Notes

1 Interview with Naguib Mahfouz, Maadi, Cairo, February 13, 2006.
2 In English, The American University in Cairo Press published *Voices from the Other World: Ancient Egyptian Tales* by Naguib Mahfouz, translated by Raymond Stock in 2002, published in paperback by Vintage Anchor in New York, 2004. *Khufu's Wisdom*, translated by Raymond Stock; *Rhadopis of Nubia*, translated by Anthony Calderbank, and *Thebes at War*, translated by Humphrey Davies, in 2003. Vintage Anchor in New York published them all in paperback in 2005, and in 2007, Alfred A. Knopf in New York brought them out as well in an omnibus edition in the Everyman's Library series entitled *Three Novels of Ancient Egypt*, introduced by Nadine Gordimer.
3 *The Cairo Trilogy* was published in Arabic in 1956–67. The American University in Cairo Press published *Palace Walk*, translated by William Maynard Hutchins and Olive E. Kenny, in 1989; *Palace of Desire*, translated by William M. Hutchins, Lorne M. Kenny, and Olive E. Kenny, in 1991, and *Sugar Street*, translated by William M. Hutchins and Angele Botros Samaan, in 1992. They published both *Cairo Modern*, translated by William M. Hutchins, in 2008, and *Khan al-Khalili*, translated by Roger Allen, in 2008. There has long been controversy over which of the latter two was actually published first, marking the change from Mahfouz's 'historical' phase to his 'realist' one.
4 Interview with Naguib Mahfouz, Maadi, December 18, 1996.
5 The description of the *ba* is from David P. Silverman, Eckley Brinton Coxe, Jr., Professor and Curator of Egyptology at the University of Pennsylvania Museum of Archaeology and Anthropology, reading a draft of this passage from an earlier work—the wording is largely his.
6 Richard B. Parkinson, *The Tale of Sinuhe and other Ancient Egyptian Poems*, 1940–1640 BC (Oxford: Oxford University Press, 1998; first published 1997), 152.

   Lucian, Vol. VII, translated by M.D. MacLeod (London: William Heinemann Ltd., and Cambridge, MA, Harvard University Press, 1961), 3.

   John Rodenbeck, "Literary Alexandria," in *The Massachusetts Review*, special Egypt issue guest-edited by Raymond Stock (Amherst: Winter 2002, 542; article, 524–72.

   Anthony Gottlieb, *The Dream of Reason: A History of Philosophy from the Greeks to the Renaissance* (London: Penguin Books, 2001), 218.

   Fu'ad Dawwarah, *Najib Mahfuz: Min al-qawmiya ila al-'alamiya* (Cairo: al-Hay'a al-'Amma al-Misriya li-l-Kitab, 1989), 197. Here Mahfouz says that he stopped going to the theater altogether after

he began to experience hearing trouble during a performance of
Alfred Farag's play *Hallaq Baghdad (The Barber of Baghdad)* in 1964.

7 Roger Allen, *An Introduction to Arabic Literature* (Cambridge: Cambridge
University Press, 2000), 111–12.

8 Ibid., 161–62.

For text, see John Richard Stephens, *Into the Mummy's Tomb* (New
York: Berkley Books, 2001), *pp.* 137–78. This story may be the
inspiration for the recent Hollywood films starring Ben Stiller, *A Night
in the Museum* (1 and 2). Though Mahfouz could not recall it when
asked, he acknowledged having read a great deal of Haggard's fiction
in Arabic translation, which "filled up the bookstores" in his youth.
(Raymond Stock, *A Mummy Awakens: The Pharaonic Fiction of Naguib
Mahfouz*, PhD dissertation, Philadelphia: University of Pennsylvania,
Department of Near Eastern Languages and Civilizations, 2008, 42,
n. 80, and 142–43.)

9 Tom Reiss, *The Orientalist: In Search of a Man Caught between East and
West* (London: Vintage, 2006), 290.

10 Interview with Naguib Mahfouz, Maadi, February 13, 2002.
Herman Te Velde, *Seth, God of Confusion* (Leiden: E.J. Brill, 1967),
Chapter Two, 85 (the standard reference work on Seth), and David
P. Silverman in the article, "Divinity and Deities in Ancient Egypt,"
Religion in Ancient Egypt: Gods, Myths and Personal Practice, ed. Byron
E. Shafer, authors John Baines, Leonard H. Lesko and David P.
Silverman (Ithaca, NY and London: Cornell University Press, 1991),
44. However, J. Gwynn Griffiths in his "Osiris" entry in *The Oxford
Encyclopedia of Ancient Egypt*, ed. Donald B. Redford (Cairo: The
American University in Cairo Press, 2001), Vol. 2, 615–19, places
Osiris's origins in Upper Egypt, as most early images of the god
depict him wearing the White Crown of the southern kingdom,
though this seems a minority view.

11 Bojana Mojsov, *Osiris: Death and Afterlife of a God* (Oxford: Blackwell,
2006), 33.

For Seth's prominence in the development of this concept in
monotheistic religion, Peter Stanford, *The Devil: A Biography* (New
York: Henry Holt, 1996), 20–23. See more on the sinister aspect of
Seth in Marc Étienne, *Heka: Magie et envoutement dans l'Égypte ancienne*
(Paris: Réunions des Musées Nationaux, 2000), 22–39.

12 J. Gwynn Griffiths, entry "Osiris," *Oxford Encyclopedia of Ancient
Egypt*, notes that, "Although the Pyramid Texts [afterlife texts found
in pyramids of the Fifth Dynasty] do not provide a consecutive
account of the Osiris myth, they abundantly supply in scattered
allusions the principal details about his fate and especially his

relationship with the deceased pharaoh,' who is identified with him in the underworld."

H. Te Velde, Seth, *God of Confusion*, Chapter Three, 6.

13 Vincent Arieh Tobin, *Theological Principles of Egyptian Religion*, foreword by Roland G. Bonnel (New York, Bern, Frankfurt am Main, Paris: Routledge Curzon, 2005), 22, notes that the myth was apparently only recorded in full form by the Greek biographer Plutarch, (46?–120?), probably with a Greek narrative and philosophical bias.

14 Richard H. Wilkinson, *Complete Gods and Goddesses of Ancient Egypt* (Cairo: The American University in Cairo Press, 2005), 148, describes Isis' iconography, and says, "through her great power Isis was able to function as the protector and sustainer of the deceased in the afterlife." This statement largely explains the role that Mahfouz assigns to the goddess in *Before the Throne*.

General description of Osiris Court trial scene in B. Mojsov, *Osiris*, xi. Osiris Court in the *Book of the Dead*, see Goelet, 101–35. For a harrowing account of the ordeal before the scales of Ma'at, see Dimitri Meeks and Christine Favard-Meeks, *Daily Life of the Egyptian Gods*, translated from French by G.M. Goshgarian (Ithaca and London: Cornell University Press, 1993), 142–50. For finds at Bahariya, see Zahi Hawass, *The Valley of the Golden Mummies* (Cairo: The American University in Cairo Press, 2000), and his article, "The Legend of the Pharaoh's Lost Tomb: A Tale from the Valley of the Golden Mummies," in *The Massachusetts Review* (Winter 2002), special Egypt issue, 475–88. Also, Raymond Stock, "Discovering Mummies," *Egypt Today*, July 1999, 64–69. For Osiris in other texts of the afterlife, see Bojana Mojsov, "The Ancient Egyptian Underworld in the Tomb of Sety I: Sacred Books of Eternal Life," in *The Massachusetts Review*, 489–506, and in *Osiris*, 58, 83–93. James P. Allen relates the origin and meaning of "hieroglyphs" in *Middle Egyptian: An Introduction to the Language and Culture of Hieroglyphs* (Cambridge and New York: Cambridge University Press, eleventh printing, 2007; first published 2000), noting the term is derived on the Greek for "sacred carvings," 2.

Najib Mahfuz, *Amama al-'arsh: Hiwar ma'a rijal Misr min Mina hatta Anwar al-Sadat* (Cairo: Maktabat Misr, 1983).

15 John Baines and Jaromir Malek, *Atlas of Ancient Egypt*, Revised Edition (Cairo: The American University in Cairo Press, 2005), 226.

16 Akef Ramzy Abadir, *Najib Mahfuz: Allegory and symbolism as a means of social, political and cultural criticism, 1936–1985*; PhD dissertation, Department of Near Eastern Languages and Literatures, New York

University, 1989 (Ann Arbor: University Microfilms International, 1990), 166–67.

17 Raja' al-Naqqash, *Najib Mahfuz: Safahat min mudhakkiratih wa adwa' jadida 'ala adabihi wa hayatih* (Cairo: Markaz al-Ahram li-l-Tarjama wa-l-Nashr), 176 and 178.

18 Published in Arabic as *al-'A'ish fi-l-haqiqa*, and in English, *Akhenaten: Dweller in Truth* by Naguib Mahfouz, translated by the Tagried Abu Hassabo (Cairo: The American University in Cairo Press, 1998) and by Vintage Anchor in New York in paperback in 2000. For how the ancient Egyptians might have answered this question, see Erik Hornung, translated from the German by John Baines, *Conceptions of God in Ancient Egypt: The One and the Many* (Ithaca, NY: Cornell University Press, 1982).

19 David O'Connor, "Egypt's View of 'Others,'" in *'Never Had the Like Occurred:' Egypt's View of its Past*, ed. John Tait (London: UCL Press, Institute of Archaeology, University of London, 2003), 155–85.

20 For the Pharaonist movement's views of Egypt as an empire, see Charles Wendell, *The Evolution of the Egyptian National Image: From its Origins to Ahmad Lutfi al-Sayyid* (Berkeley, Los Angeles, and London: University of California Press, 1972), 236–37, and for the movement as a whole and Mahfouz's connection to it, see R. Stock, *A Mummy Awakens*, 40–61.

21 Naguib Mahfouz's Nobel lecture, translated into English from the Arabic and delivered in both languages by Mohamed Salmawy in Stockholm, December 8, 1988, reprinted in *The Georgia Review* (Spring 1995): 220–21.

22 Interview with Naguib Mahfouz and Yoram Meital, Maadi, Cairo, March 1998.

23 For an analysis of *Before the Throne*, see Menahem Milson, *Najib Mahfuz: The Novelist-Philosopher of Cairo* (New York and Jerusalem: St. Martin's and Magnes Press, 1998, 144–53.)

24 *Children of the Alley*, translated by Peter Theroux (New York: Doubleday, 1996) and the American University in Cairo Press in paperback (Cairo, 2001), first translated by Philip Stewart as *Children of Gebelawi* (London: Heinemann, 1981).

25 Raymond Stock, "How Islamist Militants Put Egypt on Trial, *The Financial Times*, Weekend FT, March 4/5, 1995, III.

26 R. Stock, *A Mummy Awakens*, 20–21, and Ayman al-Hakim, "Najib Mahfuz mata wa huwa yuhibbu Isra'il!," *al-Idha'a wa-l-tilifizyun*, December 30, 2006, 84–85.
    Rasheed El-Enany, *Naguib Mahfouz: The Pursuit of Meaning* (London: Routledge, 1993), 210.

27 *The Day the Leader was Killed* by Naguib Mahfouz, translated by Malak
    Hashem (Cairo and New York: The American University in Cairo
    Press, 1997).
    Interview with Naguib Mahfouz by Egyptian critic Ghali Shukri in
    the magazine *al-Watan al-'arabi* (London: January 1988), 46.
28 Qur'an, *Surat al-fajr* (89: 27–30): "O soul at peace/Return unto thy
    Lord, well-pleased, well-pleasing/Enter thou among My
    servants/Enter thou My paradise" (Arthur J. Arberry, *The Koran
    Interpreted*. [Oxford: Oxford University Press, 1964, 1982]).
29 Miriam Lichtheim, *Ancient Egyptian Literature, Vol. II, The New Kingdom*
    (Berkeley: University of California Press, 1976), 165–78.

Modern Arabic Literature
from the American University in Cairo Press

Ibrahim Abdel Meguid *Birds of Amber* • *Distant Train*
No One Sleeps in Alexandria • *The Other Place*
Yahya Taher Abdullah *The Collar and the Bracelet* • *The Mountain of Green Tea*
Leila Abouzeid *The Last Chapter*
Hamdi Abu Golayyel *A Dog with No Tail* • *Thieves in Retirement*
Yusuf Abu Rayya *Wedding Night*
Ahmed Alaidy *Being Abbas el Abd*
Idris Ali *Dongola* • *Poor*
Radwa Ashour *Granada*
Ibrahim Aslan *The Heron* • *Nile Sparrows*
Alaa Al Aswany *Chicago* • *Friendly Fire* • *The Yacoubian Building*
Fadhil al-Azzawi *Cell Block Five* • *The Last of the Angels*
Ali Bader *Papa Sartre*
Liana Badr *The Eye of the Mirror*
Hala El Badry *A Certain Woman* • *Muntaha*
Salwa Bakr *The Golden Chariot* • *The Man from Bashmour*
The Wiles of Men
Halim Barakat *The Crane*
Hoda Barakat *Disciples of Passion* • *The Tiller of Waters*
Mourid Barghouti *I Saw Ramallah*
Mohamed Berrada *Like a Summer Never to Be Repeated*
Mohamed El-Bisatie *Clamor of the Lake*
Houses Behind the Trees • *Hunger*
A Last Glass of Tea • *Over the Bridge*
Mahmoud Darwish *The Butterfly's Burden*
Tarek Eltayeb *Cities without Palms*
Mansoura Ez Eldin *Maryam's Maze*
Ibrahim Farghali *The Smiles of the Saints*
Hamdy el-Gazzar *Black Magic*
Fathy Ghanem *The Man Who Lost His Shadow*
Randa Ghazy *Dreaming of Palestine*
Gamal al-Ghitani *Pyramid Texts* • *The Zafarani Files* • *Zayni Barakat*
Tawfiq al-Hakim *The Essential Tawfiq al-Hakim*
Yahya Hakki *The Lamp of Umm Hashim*
Abdelilah Hamdouchi *The Final Bet*
Bensalem Himmich *The Polymath* • *The Theocrat*
Taha Hussein *The Days* • *A Man of Letters* • *The Sufferers*
Sonallah Ibrahim *Cairo: From Edge to Edge* • *The Committee* • *Zaat*
Yusuf Idris *City of Love and Ashes* • *The Essential Yusuf Idris*
Denys Johnson-Davies *The AUC Press Book of Modern Arabic Literature*
In a Fertile Desert: Modern Writing from the United Arab Emirates
Under the Naked Sky: Short Stories from the Arab World
Said al-Kafrawi *The Hill of Gypsies*

Sahar Khalifeh *The End of Spring*
The Image, the Icon, and the Covenant • *The Inheritance*
Edwar al-Kharrat *Rama and the Dragon* • *Stones of Bobello*
Betool Khedairi *Absent*
Mohammed Khudayyir *Basrayatha*
Ibrahim al-Koni *Anubis* • *Gold Dust* • *The Seven Veils of Seth*
Naguib Mahfouz *Adrift on the Nile* • *Akhenaten: Dweller in Truth*
Arabian Nights and Days • *Autumn Quail* • *Before the Throne* • *The Beggar*
The Beginning and the End • *Cairo Modern*
The Cairo Trilogy: Palace Walk, Palace of Desire, Sugar Street
Children of the Alley • *The Day the Leader Was Killed*
The Dreams • *Dreams of Departure* • *Echoes of an Autobiography*
The Harafish • *The Journey of Ibn Fattouma* • *Karnak Café*
Khan al-Khalili • *Khufu's Wisdom* • *Life's Wisdom* • *Midaq Alley*
The Mirage • *Miramar* • *Mirrors* • *Morning and Evening Talk*
Naguib Mahfouz at Sidi Gaber • *Respected Sir* • *Rhadopis of Nubia*
The Search • *The Seventh Heaven* • *Thebes at War*
The Thief and the Dogs • *The Time and the Place*
Voices from the Other World • *Wedding Song*
Mohamed Makhzangi *Memories of a Meltdown*
Alia Mamdouh *The Loved Ones* • *Naphtalene*
Selim Matar *The Woman of the Flask*
Ibrahim al-Mazini *Ten Again*
Yousef Al-Mohaimeed *Wolves of the Crescent Moon*
Ahlam Mosteghanemi *Chaos of the Senses* • *Memory in the Flesh*
Shakir Mustafa *Contemporary Iraqi Fiction: An Anthology*
Mohamed Mustagab *Tales from Dayrut*
Buthaina Al Nasiri *Final Night*
Ibrahim Nasrallah *Inside the Night*
Haggag Hassan Oddoul *Nights of Musk*
Mohamed Mansi Qandil *Moon over Samarqand*
Abd al-Hakim Qasim *Rites of Assent*
Somaya Ramadan *Leaves of Narcissus*
Lenin El-Ramly *In Plain Arabic*
Mekkawi Said *Cairo Swan Song*
Ghada Samman *The Night of the First Billion*
Mahdi Issa al-Saqr *East Winds, West Winds*
Rafik Schami *Damascus Nights* • *The Dark Side of Love*
Khairy Shalaby *The Lodging House*
Miral al-Tahawy *Blue Aubergine* • *Gazelle Tracks* • *The Tent*
Bahaa Taher *As Doha Said* • *Love in Exile*
Fuad al-Takarli *The Long Way Back*
Zakaria Tamer *The Hedgehog*
M.M. Tawfik *Murder in the Tower of Happiness*
Mahmoud Al-Wardani *Heads Ripe for Plucking*
Latifa al-Zayyat *The Open Door*